Once again the Beattys give their readers a spirited heroine whose ideas are ahead of her time. Rosalind Broome, though a girl of gentle birth in Elizabethan England, refuses to accept traditional training in the ladylike virtues. In fact, she frequently dresses as a boy for protection whenever on a distant errand.

Her story begins when she is kidnapped on such an errand and taken to a den of thieves in London. There she is "baptized" into the fold with a tankard of ale. Fortunately, her failure as a pickpocket leads Rosalind to the alluring and forbidden world of the theater. Maintaining her boy's disguise, she joins a company of players and soon is acting feminine parts in the gentle Will's plays. Eventually, however, her actor's deception is exposed, and as Master Rosalind she is brought to a surprising confrontation with a kindred spirit, the ravaged old Queen herself.

The theater of Shakespeare, Queen Elizabeth's court, and the criminal underworld of the sixteenth century are all colorfully re-created here in this exuberant novel of historical adventure.

MASTER ROSALIND

JOHN AND PATRICIA BEATTY
MASTER ROSALIND

WILLIAM MORROW AND COMPANY   NEW YORK 1974

1   2   3   4   5   78   77   76   75   74

Library of Congress Cataloging in Publication Data

Beatty, John Louis (date)
   Master Rosalind.

   SUMMARY: A young girl disguises herself as a boy to play feminine roles in the theater of Shakespearean England.
   Bibliography: p.
   [1. Great Britain—History—Elizabeth, 1558–1603—Fiction. 2. Theater—England—Fiction]   I. Beatty, Patricia, joint author.   II. Title.
PZ7.B380543Mas   [Fic]   74-5050
ISBN 0-688-21819-9
ISBN 0-688-31819-3 (lib. bdg.)

CONTENTS

1821443

1

TOM O' BEDLAM

The gilded bed with its canopy of red velvet almost completely filled the old man's bedchamber. Its great size dwarfed both him as he lay inside and the younger man who sat beside him garbed in a long black physician's gown. The old man seemed to be sleeping. The physician was lost in thoughts of his own, staring at a flickering candle on a table beside the bed.

When he heard a cock crow dawn, the physician raised his head to look at the windows of the bedchamber. He leaned forward to pinch out the candle flame. Summer sunlight flooded through the windows in pale gold shafts across the rush-strewn floor. He sighed, got to his feet, and bending over to see into the bed called out very softly, "My lord, my lord. It is day."

The old man opened his eyes. For a moment he stared as if he did not know where he was. Then he nodded. He fumbled for the physician's hand and grabbed it, trying to raise himself up among his pillows.

"No, Lord Broome, do not distress yourself."

"I must. Hear me. My family. I have kin. They must know. They must know. I have a. . . ."

He would have gone on, but the physician interrupted him. "Be easy, my lord. I know what you want to say. You have a wedded sister in Hertfordshire, at Saint Albans, and she has a son. I remember his name. You told it to me. Adam Fenchurch. I will have him summoned at once. Rest now."

As the physician went very swiftly out of the room, he called for someone to come "attend Lord Broome." He did not look back to see his patient beating his fist weakly against the coverlet.

Not even the fat maidservant, who came in moments later, heard the old man's feeble mumblings from deep inside the bed. "No, no, you fool of a bloodletter. You would not wait to hear me out. I also have a younger brother, a clergyman. This brother has a son. It is to Oxfordshire you should send a messenger with news of my ailing. Send him to Oxfordshire, to the town of Cowley, to Pastor Broome, not to Hertfordshire and the Fenchurch son of my sister. Pastor Broome, not Fenchurch, is my heir. Summon Pastor Broome to me."

As Pastor Broome's blue-veined hand reached for the stick beside his chair, Rosalind moved closer to the door. She'd hoped she would not have to talk again to her grandfather before she left the next morning for Oxford. To continue their latest quarrel tonight her grandfather had stayed up past his bedtime.

"Girl, you are a fool," rumbled the old man in his deep voice. "Many a girl here in Cowley would go very willingly to Oxford to live with Lady Margaret. Many a maid would leave off scrubbing of pots here to serve a great lady, but not you, not my own kin. She would treat you as your birth deserves."

Rosalind knew she had something of the appearance of her paternal family—the thick straight black brows, brown eyes, and the silver-gilt hair—but she did not realize how greatly she resembled her tall, slender grandfather. Their faces were much alike for all that one was twelve and the other an old man.

As she paused in the kitchen doorway, she spoke angrily, "I do not want to serve any mistress. I do not want to serve anyone, to fetch and carry for them. If I had been born a lad, I would serve only as my father did in Spain."

Pastor Broome's words were bitter. "Aye, if you were a man you would leave me just as lightheartedly as he did, and you could die as Henry Broome did two years past, in Ireland if not in Spain. We fight in Ireland now. There seems no end to the wars there. Your father lies dead in the waters of the Spanish Bay of Cadiz. What did he find? He found death far from England." The old man slammed the stick down onto the table in front of him. "A waste, a great sorry waste of cleverness it was. I am glad you were not born a boy. You have had Latin and some Greek from me. Lady Margaret is an educated, pious woman. You have only to obey her small commands for a time. She will find a husband to suit your wit and talents. A husband will set all to rights for you and perhaps regain our fortunes."

Rosalind spoke equally bitterly. "Aye, a husband would have me obey his commands, too!" She scratched the coarse wool cloth of her gown as she raised her eyes impatiently to the ceiling of the kitchen. Her grandfather asked too much. A husband. God's wounds, she wanted no husband! To be a companion to old Lady Margaret, who spent half her time on her knees praying, God forbid! Rosalind felt the coins in the purse at her belt, the sixpence the housekeeper had given her to buy needles for her in Oxford and the other two pennies the old woman had given her for her own pleasure. She shuffled her feet, eager to be gone. Tomorrow she would have a full day away from her grandfather and his never-ending sermons.

Pastor Broome went on, made even more angry by her inattentiveness. "You forget you are a Broome and the Broomes of Sussex are noble lords. For all that we are poor here in Cowley, your kinsman, my elder brother, is a baron of the Queen. If my brother had been a forgiving man, I would have sent you to him to be raised as your rank requires. I should have sent your father before you to him, but I did not." The old man sighed. "Lord Broome would have made a fine lady of you. Ah, welladay, I could give you nothing but some learning, and that I have, though I see little use of it in you. My quarrel with my brother cannot be mended now. It was I who fought with him over nothing at all so many years ago. You have never seen him nor did your father see him. When your father was born, I wrote Lord Broome of him. My brother did not reply. Perhaps my letter never came to his hand. I was too proud to write again. Rosalind, you *must* serve Lady Margaret. I know you have the wit to do it and make a good marriage. For my friendship's sake she will do much for you."

It was Rosalind's turn now to sigh. Lady Margaret Forster. She heard the name day and night. And that of Dr. Hornsby of Corpus Christi College, Oxford. These were the two great persons her grandfather knew. Their names were on his lips constantly. But old Hornsby had his uses. Her grandfather borrowed books from the old scholar's library. As a result, she was permitted to travel back and forth between Oxford and Cowley as a beast-of-burden service. Another book lay on the table next to some cups and trenchers, which was her reason for going to Oxford and having a very welcome day to herself.

"Take the book to Dr. Hornsby in the morning," commanded the old man. "I trust my old friend will give you another book to bring to me. Then I ask that you visit Lady Margaret for an hour at least."

Gingerly Rosalind edged toward the candle-lit table and snatched up the large book. No, her grandfather did not bring the stick down on her arm again as she had feared he would. He said only, as she backed warily toward the door, "Rosalind, I am told that there scandalous folk in Oxford now. Have a care of them."

"Scandalous folk" seldom came to Cowley—not even moonmen, the Gypsies. She pricked up her ears and asked, "What folk, Grandfather?"

"Players. Common players lodging at an inn. Do not seek their devilish company." The old man waved his hand as if he were weary of the conversation. "We will speak again tomorrow night of this madness of yours not to live with Lady Margaret. It seems to be kin to that folly which afflicted your father. Before he went to Spain I know he filled your head with a prattling of glory and of London, the Queen and court. These things are not for you, a girl.

I should never have permitted you to listen to him. He disgraced me by becoming a common soldier." The old man's eyes sparkled with fury. "If you should ever disgrace me, Rosalind, do not come again to my house. I have reared you as well as I could."

"What if I do not marry at all?"

"That will disgrace me most of all," thundered the old man. "For all I know you may be the last of the Broome family, the last to bear the name. My brother, I believe, was childless, though married. My sister wed a Fenchurch of Hertfordshire. I know nothing of her and nothing of the Fenchurch family."

Rosalind yawned. The Broomes again and again. How weary she was of them and Lady Margaret and Dr. Hornsby.

At dawn Rosalind opened the old chest at the foot of her bed and took out her treasures, a brown doublet, hose, breeches, and shoes. Her father had outgrown these clothes long ago, but the everthrifty housekeeper had saved them. She had found them in his bedchamber after his death and taken them for her own. She put them on, tucked her hair under a wool cap, picked up the book, and was ready to go. Many a time she'd pretended to be a country lad and had yet to be found out. Her grandfather knew she journeyed about as a boy and disliked the idea, but there was no one else to do his errands in Oxford for him. He was too lame to go, and the housekeeper too busy. She would shift her clothing before she spoke with him again tonight.

Rosalind went swiftly through little Cowley and onto the road that led north to Oxford. Not until she had put Cowley a quarter mile behind her did she slow to a walk to enjoy the summer morning. The beauty of the day affected her as beauty always did. The book firmly under her arm, she looked admiringly at the hawthorne hedges on either side of the road. Dawn's dewdrops made them bejeweled things. The sky was milk-and-water blue; linnets caroled in the beeches. This wondrous free summer day was hers! She breathed deep of the scented air, then began to dance a morris in the road, skipping over the ruts farm carts had made. It was not yet five of the morning of her day. No one from Cowley would catch her dancing and name her "zany" as so many did. While she danced she thought with longing of the things her father had told her. She missed him much. He had tried to take the place of a mother to her, since her mother had died when she was very small. No, he had not corrupted her. He had told her wondrous tales of great people and a great city he had seen but once. She started to sing, "To London I will go. To London I will go."

The road to Oxford was a crooked one. Still singing to the linnets and the summer morning, Rosalind came dancing around a bend. And now she stopped short!

A man sat before her in the center of the road. He had a wild bush of black beard and long black hair. His dress consisted of gray rags, and his feet were wrapped in cloth even more filthy. To her amazement he was very daintily putting dirt into his mouth and chewing it. Sometimes he would spit out a twig or bit of hay.

As Rosalind's song trailed off into silence, she heard the man's chanting monotone, "Hough, for the bachelor! Merry doth he live." Out came another twig.

She went on gaping at the stranger. Of a sudden she guessed what he was—an Abraham Man, a begging madman. She had never seen an Abraham Man before. The housekeeper had warned her many times when she was small to be very wary of madmen, bear keepers, and all vagabonds. She'd seen a bearward once, leading a brown bear on a chain through Cowley. Bears sometimes devoured children, folk said. Vagabonds could be perilous. If *they* were dangerous, what of lunatics, of madmen? Rosalind moved to the side of the road and stepped forward cautiously.

The Abraham Man went on eating dirt, but now she noticed that he had swung his head to watch her from under his heavy brows. When she was some forty feet from him, she saw him get to his feet and sway from side to side exactly as the terrible bear had done. She made a swift decision, No, she would not run back to Cowley. Oxford was nearer now. The old tree she knew so well was nearer still. She stepped forward, her eyes on the man. Perhaps he would let a country boy past.

But when they were nearly abreast, the beggar suddenly stretched out his long arms. Then Rosalind began to run, not along the road but off to her right into the trees. Hare-like, she slipped in and out of narrow places, hoping to slow her pursuer, but still she could hear the lunatic running after her, his feet thudding on the ground. Hoarse cries came from his throat, "Ho, boy, Tom sees ya!"

Rosalind sprinted through the woods until she came to a little hollow. She leaped, terrified, down its narrow path and along its bottom toward a stand of oaks. One old tree here towered above the others. A glance over her shoulder showed her that the Abraham Man was coming down into the hollow after her. She headed for the tallest oak. Holding her breath to make herself as thin as possible, she slid inside the crack in its trunk, praying that no poisonous adders lived there now. Heaven be praised, she could still cramp herself into the secret place she'd used as a small girl to hide from playmates who played games with her in the woods. It was snug inside and black, but she could no longer crouch down in small-girl comfort. She'd grown too tall for that, but the tree was the refuge it had always been. She stood, her teeth chattering, as she heard the shouts of the madman diminishing in the distance. How long she remained in the tree she didn't know—long enough for a spider to accept her intrusion and stroll across her face. Another spider starting down her back drove her still trembling, out into the sunshine, where she looked warily about her. Aye, the lunatic was gone. But where? Back to the road, she suspected.

She would still go to Oxford, but she would not go by the road. She would travel cross-country. Perhaps the madman had only sought to beg from her, but then why had he chased her so far? Two things were certain, though. He had believed her to be a boy, and he'd called himself Tom.

Rosalind Broome found old gray Oxford already awakend to its day under the warm sunshine. The Abraham Man had cost her an hour of her precious freedom, she learned, as she heard the church bells striking eight o'clock. For all that it was not a market day and farmers were not bringing their sheep and geese to town, many people were busily abroad on the streets. She stopped, marking out the

spire of the University Church of Saint Mary the Virgin
and went toward it. Corpus Christi was in her path, just
south of it, cheek by jowl with Merton College. At the gate
of Corpus Christi she was directed by the porter, who also
took her for a boy, to the buff-walled Bachelors' Garden,
where she would find Dr. Hornsby at this hour.

She passed gowned students on her way. They paid no
heed to her. From their garments beneath their black
scholar's robes she could tell their place and rank. Gentlemen Commoners, the sons of noblemen, wore satin and
velvet. The Commoners dressed in stammel, as befit the
sons of merchants. As for the poor Battelers, the servants
of the richer scholars, who hurried about carrying water
and doing the bidding of better-born youths, they were
shabby as herself. A sweating Batteler ran by on an errand
for another luckier student. Aye, she might have to go to
Lady Margaret's house because she was poor, but she
would not be happy there. For all that the goodly old
woman might dress her in satin and velvet she would be
no more than a Batteler.

Dr. Hornsby, a tall heavy old man with an iron-gray
beard, walked, hands clasped behind his back, among the
flowers of the Bachelors' Garden. He nodded to Rosalind
after she had bowed, boylike, and asked, "Master Broome,
how did your grandfather like my book?" Months past Dr.
Hornsby had accepted her masquerade as a boy when she'd
informed him that her grandfather could not come to Oxford himself and that a boy could journey more safely than
a girl. He always called her Master Broome in a special
tone. And Rosalind saw the mocking dagger in the name.

"He did not tell me, sir, but he bade me ask you to lend
him another," said Rosalind, giving him the book.

To her horror the old scholar glared at her. "In a letter he sent last week I was told by your grandfather that you have fallen into folly, too, and do not want to live at Lady Margaret's house."

Rosalind swallowed hard. She was terrified of Hornsby's flaming rages. He had even scolded Queen Elizabeth to her face at one time. He put his hand on her shoulder. "Your only future lies in a good marriage. Your father is dead. Your grandfather is very old and has little time more. Go to Lady Margaret. But now go to my chamber and ask my servant for my new book from London, the red book. Take it home to your grandsire. And do not tarry long here in Oxford today. I am told there are strange evil folk about—players and vagabonds."

Rosalind knew she was dismissed. Happy to have escaped so easily from two terrible men that day, she left the Bachelor's Garden, ran across the green garden of Nevill's Inn, and climbed the steps of Urban Hall to Hornsby's lodgings. There an old manservant gave her another book, this time a larger, finer one bound in scarlet velvet. Then, like a well-sent arrow, she ran back to the gate. Her mood was rebellious. She had had enough of old men in the last two days—old men who were set upon planning her life for her. It was her life, not theirs. She paused just outside the college. The doting housekeeper had given her some pennies for bread, beer, and cheese at midday, and if it cost no more than a penny, she was going to see the wicked players perform their play. That disobedience would pay her grandfather and Hornsby, too, for their unwelcome lecturing.

Rosalind loitered near the gate until two scholars strolled out. Oxford scholars would know what inn lodged players. They knew all of the news of the old town. She greeted them with a cheery, "Where can I find the players, good sirs?"

Both were Gentlemen Commoners. They looked at her coldly, then one said, "At the White Swan, booby, at three of the clock."

She rankled to be named a booby. She was no more fool than they, and her manners were better. Mockingly she asked them, "And what must I pay, good sirs?"

"A penny if you have one, boy," said the second scholar.

"I have a penny, and more," she flared and turned her back on them, leaving them laughing at her. "If I'd been a man," she muttered, as she stalked away, "I would have taught them better manners with a blade."

Rosalind knew the innkeeper's wife at the White Swan from other visits to Oxford. She was a plump woman, who brought her the food she ordered for her penny, and more —even a fair slab of boiled mutton. The innkeeper was busy serving player folk in a private chamber, the woman confided to Rosalind, sitting down across from her. The woman seemed oddly eager to talk, and Rosalind also noted that her face today was glum, not jolly. "I do not know that we have done aright in permitting strolling players at our inn."

"Are they greatly wicked?" asked Rosalind. She had strained her ears to hear sounds from the private chamber but had heard nothing except some very loud laughter and no interesting new oaths at all.

The woman shook her head. "No more than any other men who travel on the roads these days. Their play has been licensed by the council and the bailiffs. The players

pay my husband well enough for lodging and the use of
our innyard. But townsfolk rail against them, boy, saying
they are a scandal to Oxford and masterless men, because
players have no guild of their own. Scholars who dare come
here to see a play can be flogged if they are caught by a
schoolmaster."

Rosalind had not known this delicious piece of information. "I am no scholar," she boasted. Having been taken
once more for a boy made her play the part of one. "I am
going to see a play before I become a soldier and go soon
to serve under the great Earl of Essex as my father did."

The innkeeper's wife swallowed the lie. "Aye, many folk
who travel here speak of Essex. He is the greatest lord in
all England, the old Queen's favorite."

"My father died at Cadiz in Spain for the Queen," put
in Rosalind. The woman's comment about folk who travel
made her think of the Abraham Man, so she asked, "Has
there been a madman about, goodwife?"

The woman threw up her apron in disgust. "So you have
seen him too? A fierce fellow, he is. The constables beat
him about the head with sticks last night and sent him on
his way out of town. I gave him bread at sunset to escape
his curse on our inn, hoping to make him go away and
leave us in peace. But he would not. He pushed me aside
and went in to sit at our hearth next to our guests. Sometimes he sang to himself, but that is not what frightened me
most." The woman leaned closer to Rosalind. "My husband saw it also. The lunatic now and then seemed to listen
to men's private talk. I saw him move his stool nearer gossiping folk twice. 'Tis said at other inns he has been caught
listening at closed doors." She mused. "He did no one any

harm, but I was forced to summon the constables to take him out from here and beat him. He would not go otherwise. And you have seen him? Is he in Oxford still?"

"No, dame. He chased me on the road from Cowley."

The woman's eyes widened. "Lord be praised, you got away from him. Take care, boy. He chased no soul here. Who knows what a moonstruck man will do? He might have murdered you. Lunatics should not be abroad, God knows. They are a danger to all."

Until near three o'clock by the church bells Rosalind strolled along the banks of the Cherwell and Isis, watching fishermen. Then she made her way again to the White Swan. There she gave her penny to the innkeeper's wife and entered the innyard. Little was to be seen except for a platform made of boards with a red curtain drawn across its back under the inn gallery. The yard today was bare of carts and well swept. Rosalind would have sat toward the back rows of benches brought out for the performance, but in the first row she saw the two Corpus Christi Gentlemen Commoners who had been rude to her. She moved up behind them to sit within earshot. Perhaps they would speak of London or the Queen?

She heard the first scholar say, "You are London-bred. Alas, I was reared in savage Northumberland. You have seen plays in London Town."

"Indeed I have," came the preening answer. The other youth gestured in contempt toward the makeshift stage. "I have seen far better theaters and better plays than the old one we see today. It is not heroic."

Rosalind drank in this tidbit eagerly. She felt very daring, enjoying what was forbidden, and would have gone on eavesdropping, but the London-born scholar spoke more softly now that Oxford's citizens began to crowd into the innyard.

At three o'clock the benches were filled and latecomers were standing crowded close together. Then the curtain parted and out stepped a red-jerkined trumpeter, who blew an off-key blast, bowed, and went back through the curtains. After him came a small bearded man who mumbled a prologue. Then the play began. Within five minutes Rosalind was totally captured by it. She laughed at the loud-mouthed hero, the conceited booby, who claimed that "many women" loved him. She laughed even harder when the serving maids of the pert widow he had chosen as his sweetheart struck him over the head. Lost in a world she had never known existed, she did not notice that the players' costumes were shabby and some of the actors drunken. Two swayed and lurched about, delivering their lines badly. One even fell down and rolled off the stage, but Rosalind thought it was part of the comedy. She knew only that she had never before so enjoyed anything. The play held her so completely that she forgot who she was or where she was or that she was doing a forbidden thing.

A furious bellowing brought her wits abruptly back to the White Swan and her own danger. The roaring came from the throat of Dr. Hornsby. His face purple, the old man came hurtling through the startled citizens, his arms outstretched. He was headed directly for her. Rosalind and the Gentlemen Commoners scrambled up at the same moment. "Run!" cried one scholar, as Hornsby's right hand clamped down on his shoulder and his left reached for the other youth and caught him too.

Snatching up the book beside her, Rosalind dove into

the laughing crowd and into the street. She felt safe there for a moment, but as she paused to get her bearings, she heard her name shouted. "You, Rosalind! Your grandfather will hear of this. I saw you. I promise you."

Then she ran again and didn't stop until she'd reached the outskirts of Oxford and was on the road to Cowley. When she could run no more, she threw herself down beside a hedge, sobbing for breath.

Suddenly without warning, without a sound, a long arm came writhing through the hedge and wrapped itself about her neck. At the same instant Rosalind felt the hard point of a dagger in her ribs. Terrified, she stared up through a gap in the hawthorne into the face of the man who held her. It was the Abraham Man, and the madman was smiling.

"I'll have that," said the lunatic, removing the dagger and snatching the book from under her arm. With a laugh, he let her go, pushing her forward onto her knees. She got to her feet as quickly as she could but found the beggar, who had rolled under the hedge even more swiftly, standing over her, the book in his hands as he thumbed the pages. His dagger was back in its sheath on his right hip. He looked at Rosalind, then laughed at the look of disbelief on her face.

"You are not mad?" she quavered.

"No more than any other man in England, my lad."

Rosalind pointed to the book. "It is not mine, sir."

"No, it is mine now. It will bring me a good sum—perhaps two golden crowns, I think. The author is well known in London. His books fetch a good price."

Rosalind's mouth hung open. The Abraham Man not

only could read, he must be well educated. What manner
of man was he? She stammered, "But, sir, I am to take the
book to my grandfather in Cowley. The book is Dr. Hornsby's."

The Abraham Man eyed Rosalind, grinning as he put
the book into the rags at his breast. "I saw you coming
from Cowley. You'll not go there again and tell the constables that poor Tom o'Bedlam stole the great Dr. Hornsby's book. I will not be beaten again in Oxfordshire this
time." The man reached out and caught her by the ear and
forced her ahead of him along the road and through a
bigger gap in the hedge. Still holding her fast and painfully,
the beggar told her, "You'll be my tongue for two days' time
till we reach London. If you don't choose to have your ear
pulled off, you'll come with me gently, and you'll make no
outcry to any village constable you see."

Bewildered and terrified, Rosalind was hastened cross-
country by her captor. He seemed to know the cowpaths of
Oxfordshire as well as she. They avoided all sight of folk
she might know as they slipped through hedges, over
meadows, and passed under trees. After a time her wits re-
gathered, and she wondered why his haste? It was almost
as if the Abraham Man had business that was urgent. He
seemed bent on speed until they reached High Wycombe,
and there he forced her to beg for her "poor mad uncle."
With the pennies pitying villagers gave her, they bought
food at an inn and spent that night unseen in a farmer's
hayloft. The Abraham Man slept soundly while Rosalind
lay weeping silently into the prickly, unfeeling hay. She
could not get away. Tom o'Bedlam had tied her hand and
foot with a rope the farmer used to lead his cows to market.

Rosalind was grateful for one thing only—that he had accepted her totally as a lad.

She walked quietly with him the next day, frightened that in pulling her ear once again, he might pull off the cap that concealed her long hair.

That night they spent at an inn not far outside small Uxbridge. Rosalind thought the Abraham Man seemed very well known to the innkeeper. He did not even pretend to be mad as they boldly entered the inn's kitchen. The innkeeper greeted him with, "Ah, Tom o' Bedlam, what news have ye this time?" Then he put charneco wine before the Abraham Man and a bowl of porridge with cream before Rosalind. As she ate, she thought how odd that all of the other innkeepers they had seen since they left the Cowley road had been very hostile to them. They had sold food to her and taken the sixpence for the needles, but at once barred their doors when Tom had pushed her forward as if they would both go to the hearth.

Tom's reply as he lifted his goblet seemed a strange one. "The blue crane's bill blooms still this summer. I found little loosestrife as yet on the banks of the rivers."

The innkeeper nodded thoughtfully and replied even more strangely, "The flowers of the pimpernel stay open in the cornfields, though."

Rosalind thought it odd when she was shown to a pleasant bedchamber with a good bed and fine nettle linen sheets. She had no idea where Tom o' Bedlam had got to. That night she awoke in the summer moonlight to voices outside her door in the hallway. She crept to the door to listen, knowing it had been bolted by Tom from the outside.

"What does the lad with you know of our business, Tom?" Rosalind heard the innkeeper ask in a suspicious, hissing voice.

The Abraham Man answered, "Nothing. I have told him nothing save that I am not mad. I do not serve the Devil every moment any more than you do. At times I serve myself. The book is worth money to me. What matters between the boy and me is that he does not tell who stole the book. He may have his uses as a kyncheon cove in London. I take him to the Upright Man."

"Will you seek another audience there with the Devil?"

"I see him seldom as I can. 'Tis for the Upright Man to go to the Devil and take me along as he chooses. He is my master first. Then the Devil."

"God give you good night, Tom," said the innkeeper. Rosalind heard the door next to hers shut and, some minutes later, Tom's snoring. Shivering, she went back to bed wondering who the Upright Man was and what a kyncheon cove might be. Tears stung her eyes. No one in Cowley or Oxford had seen her with the Abraham Man. Her grandfather would hear from Dr. Hornsby that she had gone to a forbidden play and had taken the book with her. They would think she had run away with it. They would believe that she would do such a thing rather than go to Lady Margaret's house.

At dawn Rosalind and Tom o' Bedlam started on their way to London with a gift from the innkeeper, roast beef and bread tied in a napkin in Tom's clothing. At the kitchen door she heard the Abraham Man's whispered question, another strange one. "Have you heard gossip from them of the red witch and the Devil?" He jerked his thumb toward the common room, where three merchants who had come in late the night before broke their morning fast.

"Naught but what every man knows. Godspeed to London, Tom."

Rosalind walked along, her head hanging. As she trudged beside Tom, she thought of him and of the innkeeper. A clever beggar who pretended to be a madman and a country innkeeper who welcomed him! Two men who spoke of devils and flowers and witches. She could make nothing of any of it except that she felt they were not fools. There was an air of danger about them.

Brentford in Middlesex was little more than a village, too, but it was the Abraham Man's destination. There, as if he owned the country and need fear no constables, he went striding across green meadows and before houses. Some dwellings she saw were mere huts, others goodly three-storied timber houses with thatched roofs. It was to one of these, a house close to the river Thames, that Tom o' Bedlam took her. He poked her in the ribs as they stood beside a red lattice beneath a huge sign. On it she saw a crudely painted white lamb with yellow sunrays surrounding it.

"'Tis the Holy Lamb where we'll find the Upright Man. Because you are such poor meat, I trust he'll not slit your throat on the spot." Tom laughed and, seizing her shoulders, pushed her ahead of him through the inn's heavy dark doors.

11

THE UPRIGHT MAN OF LONDON

At that same moment in Saint Albans in the county of
Hertfordshire, some thirty miles from the Holy Lamb, the
swarthy, sharp-faced manservant opened the upper casement window at his master's command. "Look out, Martin.
Is it the courier?"

Martin Sclater stuck out his sleek head of black hair,
stared at the man on horseback below, and said, "No, Master Fenchurch, it is a stranger. Who are you?" he shouted
down to the rider.

The answer came floating up to the window. "I've come
from Sussex, from Lord Broome's house. He lies a-dying
and wishes Mistress Alys Fenchurch, his sister, to know of
this."

Adam Fenchurch got up from the table, where he was
writing. He came to the window, pushed Sclater aside, and
cried down, "My mother was Mistress Fenchurch. She died
a year ago."

"Then the message is for you, Master Fenchurch."

"Martin," Fenchurch ordered, "bring the messenger into
the house and serve him wine. But first close the window."

"Yes, master." As Sclater pulled the window shut with powerful but horribly scarred hands, Fenchurch went back to his papers.

Fenchurch said to the servant, "My letter can wait an hour before the courier comes for it. I have time to see this messenger who comes to me. God's blood, my ancient uncle is dying at last. Who would have thought my mother would die before him, and she fifteen years younger than he."

Fenchurch stood, his thumb to his teeth, shaking his yellow head, his dark eyebrows drawn together in a frown. Then he flicked dust from one elbow of his green doublet, laughed, and went downstairs after Sclater to greet the messenger.

The red-faced messenger took a sip of wine with gratitude, then told Fenchurch, "In truth, master, it is Lord Broome's physician who sent me with the message. Lord Broome is abed and cannot write you. He can scarce speak at all. The physician bids me tell you that he believes Lord Broome considers a Fenchurch to be his heir. Lord Broome's children, all four, died before him."

"And I am the only Fenchurch." The fair-haired man nodded with satisfaction. "When I have settled some business I have here in Saint Albans, I will ride to my uncle's house in Sussex. Do you think the old man will live some days longer?"

The messenger shook his head. "Master Fenchurch, I do not know that. I am not a physician. I do not know how Lord Broome fares now. Perhaps he died while I rode here to you."

"Aye, perhaps. I will come as quickly as I can. Thank

you for coming to me." Fenchurch spoke to Sclater. "Martin, give this man another cup of wine and a crown for his trouble. Then come above to me again."

Upstairs once more Fenchurch went back to his quill and paper, but he didn't begin to write. He sat at the table smiling, then said to himself, "It seems I am to become the Baron of Broome. It is something I fancy. My uncle, according to my mother, was rich in lands and flocks of sheep."

After the messenger had gone, Sclater came upstairs and stood beside the door. Fenchurch pointed at him and said, laughing, "How would you like to serve a noble lord, Martin?"

Sclater smiled thinly. "Master, I have served the Fenchurch family for twenty-five years. Sometimes in her last ailment your mother spoke to me of the Broomes, her people. You may not be the heir to the barony."

"No? How is that?" Fenchurch looked startled.

"There were three Broomes. Lord Broome, your mother, and a younger brother to Lord Broome."

"I did not know of him!"

The servant nodded. "He quarreled with Lord Broome as a young man, and your mother took Lord Broome's part in the matter. Your mother never saw her other brother again. She and Lord Broome made a compact never to speak his name again. I do not know if the younger brother lives still, or where he lives. He was but two years younger than Lord Broome. He may have wed. He may have sons or a daughter. Even if only a daughter, she would be the legal heir to the barony."

Fenchurch closed his fist slowly on a sheet of paper. He

asked, "And did my mother tell you where this younger brother was when she last heard of him?"

"No, master. But he is named Broome. And he will be very old. Perhaps he is dead, too, and was childless."

"Perhaps, Martin."

The servant came over to his master. Picking up the same word, he said, "Perhaps the Devil will know somewhat of this younger brother. I have never heard his Christian name. When the courier comes from London, why not send a second letter with him? It will be from you asking of the family of Lord Broome."

"Yes, the Devil could know." Fenchurch threw the crumpled paper onto the floor, pulled a new sheet to him, and started to write.

Sclater stood behind him, looking over his shoulder. He said, "If the brother or some of his children can be found, shall I visit them for you, Master Fenchurch?"

"Aye, Martin, you shall visit them, You will bring them fond greetings from their loving Cousin Fenchurch. I think your dagger will do best."

Because the day had been bright, Rosalind's eyes had to adjust to the dark slowly, but her sniffing nose told her that she scented ale, tobacco, roast meat, old dirt, and the stench of rank grease. But there was a strange grace note, too, the perfume of midsummer roses. A man's roar came as if across a large room as she waited beside the Abraham Man. Then the Abraham Man repeated the same ridiculous words that he had addressed to the innkeeper the night before. "The blue crane's bill blooms still this summer. I found little loosestrife as yet on the banks of the rivers," he shouted.

This time nothing was said in return about "pimpernels." Instead the voice bellowed, "What have ye fetched here with ye, Tom?"

"A boy. I found him along the road, found him with a book I will sell. He could make a nip."

"Bring him to me."

Propelled by the Abraham Man, Rosalind staggered across the great hearth. She could see now that she was in the common room of a tavern, a rather ordinary sort of room with tables, benches, and many three-legged stools. There were perhaps a dozen people in the Holy Lamb, lolling at their ease at the tables, tankards and jacks of ale before them. One man, though, had a choice place before the hearth. With him sat a woman, whose hair gleamed black-red in the firelight.

Tom o' Bedlam took Rosalind before these two and whacked her on the back. "Bow to the Upright Man of London, lad."

Afraid, Rosalind bowed, then lifting her head stared into the Upright Man's face. It was long like a horse's, dark-skinned, heavy-boned, and marked with the pits of smallpox. His hair was brown and lank-straight. His clothing that she could see above the tabletop was very fine, a silken doublet of lusty, gallant red. His ruff was large and pleated and in his ear a dangling pearl. She saw him touch the woman's arm, drawing her attention to Rosalind. Hers was a sharp face with pointed chin and slanting eyes. Her gown was russet as a ripe leatherjacket apple and shimmered the color of Catherine pear. As she moved toward Rosalind, the scent of rose water came drifting from her.

"What are ye called?" she asked Rosalind.

"Robin, my lady." Rosalind gave the name she always

used when she masqueraded as a lad. It was near in sound to Rosalind but a boy's name.

Wild laughter rang out in the common room. One man called out, " 'My lady'? Our Moll Cutpurse?"

"Hold your clack," roared the Upright Man. "Moll is my sweeting. All honest canting men must have a care of the honor of the Upright Man's woman." Then he spoke to Rosalind. "So ye would become a nip?"

"Moll can tell the lad," said Tom o' Bedlam. "I saw no cause to say what it is on the road. 'Tis not my trade—nipping."

In a sweet low voice Moll Cutpurse explained to Rosalind, "A nip lightens gentlemen's purses. He takes coins out of them with his fingers, and they do not know it."

"But, my lady, that is against the Queen's law. That is stealing!" blurted Rosalind, shocked.

If she had thought calling Moll "my lady" had entertained the company of the Holy Lamb, this last remark entertained them far more. They howled for a full minute until the Upright Man, who was also laughing, banged on the table with his pewter cup to bring them to order. When they were still grinning but silent, he did an extraordinary thing. He took up his tankard and leaning forward over the table poured its whole contents, near a full quart, over Rosalind's unsuspecting head.

He said, "I baptize ye one o' us, Robin. Tom, do ye stand godfather to him?"

"Aye, so I do stand godfather," vowed the Abraham Man.

"Moll, do ye stand godmother and ye will undertake his training?"

"Aye, Upright Man."

Soaked to the skin, Rosalind was too shocked to say a word. She could only gasp, lick ale dripping down from about her mouth with her tongue, and listen dazed to the Upright Man's next words. "Here is our catechism for a canting man. You can hang in England for cutting a purse, or taking a farthing from a man. You can hang for murder, for clipping a coin for its gold, robbing on the high road, for taking a cow from her meadow or a horse to Scotland, or for stealing hawk's eggs. You are now a canting man, Robin—a 'rogue' some call us. Some of us will hang. Others the Devil looks after. . . ."

A little man who sat nearby interrupted, growling. "The Devil does not see to all things to repay us for what we do for him, Upright Man. Nineteen rogues were hanged at Tyburn Gallows not long past."

"And so they were because they were caught. The Devil does not see to small matters," said the leader of the canting men. He grinned as he suddenly leaned over the table once more. Grabbing Rosalind's cap before she knew what he planned to do, he pulled it off. As her long hair fell to her waist, he shouted, "A wench! Tom o' Bedlam has brought us a wench and said he brought a lad." He doubled over with laughter.

Her hair matted with ale and hanging in strings, Rosalind heard the Abraham Man's bellow of anger. "I knew it was a wench from the first moment!"

"No, Tom, we heard ye. Ye did not," came from Moll.

The Upright Man stabbed a finger at Tom. "No, ye did not, Tom. I can see it in your face."

A white-haired woman with a patch over one eye

slammed down her ale and cackled. "The wench gulled clever Tom. We heard ye say ye brought a lad to Moll." She slapped her hands on her knees. "Tom o' Bedlam gulled. What will the Devil say to that? Tom does not know a wench from a lad."

Tom thundered, "He'll not hear of it. What is this girl to him? Ye'll not tell him, nor will she."

Rosalind looked to her right. Tom's face was red with anger, veins standing out on his forehead as he clutched his hands together. He had been made a fool of and he was furious.

"Boy or girl, it's all the same to me," said Moll. "I've stood godmother to her."

"And like it or no, Tom, you've stood godfather," added the Upright Man. "The girl is Moll's. There'll be no trouble because of her."

"Under my favor she is," said Moll. She got up, came around the table, took Rosalind by the hand, and led her to a bench set sideways to the fire. As they went Rosalind looked fearfully over her shoulder and saw the Upright Man pushing a grumbling Tom o' Bedlam toward an empty table.

"Pay them no heed," Moll told Rosalind. "They are often like this. The Upright Man has more important business now with Tom. We have waited long for him to return. Where is your home, girl? And do not tell me again you are named Robin."

"No, my lady, I am Rosalind Broome. I live in Cowley, in Oxfordshire."

"Who is your father?"

Rosalind liked the beautiful woman, who smelled of roses and wore silver shears hanging from a silken cord about her waist. She told her of her father's death in Spain, then of her pastor grandfather. As they talked, a huge yellow cat, a gib cat by the scars of battle on him, leaped from somewhere out of the room's shadows onto Moll's lap. While he purred Rosalind spoke of the play she'd watched, of Dr. Hornsby's fury, and of the stolen book. She finished with, "And it please you, my lady, give me back my cap and I will go home now. I will tell my grandfather that a beggar stole the book and dragged me to London with him. I will not tell him it was Tom o' Bedlam. Tom can have the book."

Moll gave Rosalind a strange crooked smile. "I cannot send you from here. You cannot go home. The Upright Man has baptized ye. Ye must be one of us now. Ye belong to me. There are girls in my household working for me." She jerked her head toward Tom o' Bedlam. "Do not think to run away. In a week's time there'll not be a rogue in London Town who will not know ye and the tale of how ye gulled Tom. He is a man of great pride. Rosalind, ye made him play the fool. He may not forgive ye for it, and he may welcome the chance to pay ye out for it."

Rosalind stuttered, "I meant him no harm. I was afraid of him. I did not speak to him at all if I could help it."

"I know that. In time Tom may grow to know it also. But ye'll be safest from him with me in my house in Whitefriars. Now, Rosalind, there is much you must learn to be a kyncheon cove."

"What are they, my lady?" 1821443

"Rogue children."

The remainder of that long day Moll spent teaching more of the thieves' speech to Rosalind. She learned of the rogues she saw in the Holy Lamb. Each had a different name for the criminal work he did. The ruffler, a one-armed man, who claimed he had once been a brave soldier of the Queen, begged alms for his honorable wounds. His drinking companion today was a prigger of prauncers, a horse thief. At another table sat a tall thin woman who was an angler, a female rogue who stole goods out of shops. The tall handsome man across from her was a high lawyer, or highwayman. A forger, or jackman, got up when summoned by the Upright Man and went over to speak with him and Tom. Others of the Holy Lamb's rogues were common thieves, who turned their hands to anything profitable, Moll explained.

"And everyone here serves the Devil?" Rosalind asked, though her grandfather had warned her many times over never to speak the evil one's name aloud for fear he might feel summoned.

"What do you know of him?" asked Moll.

"I heard Tom say that he served the Devil." Rosalind looked at Moll in sudden fright. "Can you weep?" she asked. All the talk of the Devil and Moll's liking for her gib cat made her think of witches. Witches favored cats. Witches who served the Devil could not weep. And Moll's hair was red. Was she the red witch the Abraham Man had spoken of?

Moll said sharply, "I am no witch, and there are no wizards among us, though some pretend to be to gull simple folk. Some of us serve the Devil as we once served his failing father before him. We fell heir to the Devil." Rosalind saw her shiver.

"His father?" Rosalind had never heard that the Devil had a father, much less a "failing one."

"No more of such clack. Do not speak of the Devil. 'Tis

not wise. Tonight I take you with me to my house. There you will go to my school on Smart's Quay."

"I read and write, my lady."

"Ye'll read no books at my house. And ye will never be lonely. There are others there, my kyncheon coves, to teach you London ways and what you must know. Are you hungry, Rosalind?"

"Aye, my lady."

All that day the Upright Man and Tom o' Bedlam conferred quietly. At sunset Tom went abovestairs. There he remained long. When he came down he was so clean and well clad that Rosalind scarcely knew him. His hair and beard were trimmed and combed to neatness. His doublet and breeches were of pease-porridge tawny, his hose of primrose yellow. At his side he wore a silver-hilted sword, the twin of the Upright Man's. Together the two rogues came to Moll, and the Upright Man bent to kiss her. "A good night, sweeting," he told her. "When the girl's been made a rogue, fetch her to me and I'll judge her work."

Moll's voice was tender-soft though her words were not. "Pigsnye, go you now to the Devil and see that he pays you golden angels for your work."

That night, half asleep on the high seat of Moll's cart, Rosalind Broome entered London. Moll, the cat on her lap, sat next to her as the rogue who drove the cart wound through the narrow, black streets of the old city. Rosalind scarcely heard the cry of the watch in the distance as the carter pulled to a stop in Whitefriars.

> Give ear to the clock!
> Beware your lock!
> Your fire and your light!

And God give you good night!
One o'clock.

With Moll's help she went into a house and upstairs and fell sleepily onto the bed toward which the woman shoved her.

Rosalind awoke to the cries of the city. A man was selling hats in the street below, by the sound of his bawling, and a woman's voice rose above his deeper one as she sang out, "Hot lamb pies. Hot mutton pies. Fresh from the baking."

As soon as she'd rubbed the sleep out of her eyes, Rosalind noticed that she had a bedfellow, a tiny pinch-faced child no more than six years old. The girl-child, who wore a kersey gown, flung back a tattered coverlet and sat up, yawning. She looked unsmiling and unsurprised at Rosalind. "I'll take ye to Dickon. He's master of the kyncheon coves."

Rosalind asked, "Who is Dickon?"

"Come wi' me." The child got up and led the way downstairs.

At the foot of the stairs Rosalind saw a thin ragged boy with a tangle of reddish hair, a freckled face, and small bright eyes.

"'Tis Dickon," said the child.

"There's food fer us in the kitchen," Dickon stated abruptly. Then he added, "I'm a nip. Moll says I'm to take ye to Smart's Quay today after ye've shifted to wench's garb."

Rosalind looked about her as she went through the

house to the kitchen. The room she'd shared with the little girl had been a poor one with naught in it but a bed. Moll's house did not seem fine to her, though she saw handsome pieces of furniture in some of the rooms, stolen goods waiting for a buyer, she later learned. As she, Dickon, and the child went along a sour-smelling passageway, a large black rat skittered across their path and out the open side door into a heap of rubbish piled in front of the house. A tall black-haired, brown-faced girl in a ragged gown came through the door an instant after the rat and stood staring at Rosalind, a basket of fish under her arm. "She's one o' us, a kyncheon cove. She's to be an angler, Helen is," explained Dickon.

In Moll's dirty kitchen the rogue children were fed by an old crone with unbound gray hair. She gave Rosalind, the small child, Dickon, Helen, and two other boys younger than Dickon porridge, salt herring, and small beer. The little rogues ate and drank with haste. So did Rosalind, copying them.

When they were finished, the old woman mumbled to Rosalind, "Ye'll find kirtle and bodice and petticoat for ye in the basket by the hearth."

Rosalind took the basket upstairs and changed into girl's clothing but kept her shoes, as those provided for her were too small. Then she came below to be met by Dickon and the old woman who said to him, "Look to it, Dickon. The girl is favored by Moll. She names Moll 'my lady.' Moll likes that."

"Hold your clack," said Dickon, as he motioned for the other children to follow him. Because she saw no alternative, Rosalind brought up the rear of the procession of kyncheon coves. But at a signal from Dickon one of the smaller boys waited for her to pass, then dropped into line behind her. She was being watched.

The houses on Moll's lane were narrow two-story wooden ones, standing close together, with their upper stories projecting out over the footpath, blocking out the sunlight. Their window glass was cheap and thick and their roofs of straw. Half-starved dogs slunk along the path, nosing about hopefully in the stinking rat-infested refuse heaps. On top of one heap stood Moll's yellow cat, his back arched as he hissed at a bold dog. Poorly dressed, hollow-cheeked men and women passed by the children, who headed toward the Thames. One or two nodded to the strutting Dickon and looked curiously at Rosalind in her faded and ripped brown bodice and black kirtle.

The kyncheon coves entered a low shed built on a wharf over the Thames. The rag-clad doorkeeper was a beggar, too, who had inflicted sores on his bare arms. As the Queen's penalty for crime, holes had been bored through the gristle of both his ears. The man was a clapperdud-geon, someone who had wounded himself in order to create sympathy for his plight. After opening the door to Dickon's low whistle, he at once slammed it behind the children and bolted it. Rosalind stared around her. She was in a most strange place. Long wooden and iron hooks were stacked against bare walls near tables of jumbled clothing and rags strewn on ropes. Directly before her she saw a remarkable apparatus hanging from a beam. From it were suspended a black velvet purse and what seemed to be a leather sack. Both sack and purse had metal counters and tiny silver hawk's bells sewed on them. Over the sack and the purse as well hung larger sacring bells.

Moll came swaying in her russet gown, a medlar fruit in her hand. "Dickon, show Rosalind what ye do."

Rosalind watched the boy go carefully and swiftly as the woman's cat to the purse, open it, and reach gingerly into it without the clicking of a counter or the tinkle of one bell and haul out a twinkling golden coin, an angel.

"Now, Rosalind, ye try it," ordered Moll. "Nip into the purse."

Rosalind pushed back her hair and reached cautiously toward the purse. To her horror, she misjudged her aim and the distance, making every bell jingle merrily.

Flinging her medlar to Dickon, Moll said, "A nip's not made overnight. Ye can try again, Rosalind, but now I have business with Helen." She sent the dark-faced girl to take down a hook, and as she expertly demonstrated to Helen how one angled with it for a linen petticoat thrown over the rope as if drying on a line or hedge, she called out over her shoulder to Dickon, "Take Rosalind about the town. Have her see how ye and the jostler work."

Dickon's eyes lit up at the prospect. He threw Moll's medlar to a younger lad, gestured to Rosalind to follow him, and together with another kyncheon cove, a shock-headed, blunt-nosed boy of about nine, they were let out by the surly, cursing clapperdudgeon.

"Have ye seen London Town afore?" asked Dickon.

"No."

Dickon explained with great pride, "The Thames be London's high road. See the wherries and barges on it." He gestured. "This would be Whitefriars now. Would ye like to see the old Queen's palace and rich Blackfriars and Essex House, where the great earl lives in London?"

Rosalind nodded with happy relief. Smart's Quay had

frightened her but London Town did not. She followed eagerly as Dickon walked ahead, weaving in and out of the crowds, avoiding porters who lurched along carrying burdens on their backs, water carriers, balladmongers, and street peddlers. Carts and wains were everywhere, blocking the way, as were caroches, tiny coaches that carried one lady only. Rosalind spied out an old woman with green jewels in her ears in one of them. "Is that the Queen?" she asked Dickon.

"Na, she's gone from London. Summer is plague time. She comes back ter Whitehall Palace or Greenwich Palace come November. After Candlemas she goes outa the city again."

The three stepped over the carcass of a dead dog in the middle of the street. As they did, they disturbed ravens, which lifted off, scolding them, and flapped down on a church spire a distance away.

All morning and late into the afternoon Dickon and his jostler and Rosalind toured London. Rosalind watched gallants hand farthingaled ladies out of watermen's boats up the slippery river stairs at the wharves at Queen's Hythe. The wherrymen's musical shouts of "Eastward Ho, Westward Ho," rang in her ears as she gaped at the fine stone houses of the Queen's lords, which lined the north bank of the river. The nip led her next to Whitehall Palace. Rosalind was fascinated by the monstrous mass of brick and was astounded that she and every other humble person could stroll about the flower-filled gardens behind it and under its archway as if they, not the Queen, owned it.

Later, while she craned her neck to look overhead into the high vault of Westminster Abbey, Dickon poured into her unhappy ears things he thought she must know about her future profession as a rogue.

"Have a care of the City Watch," he said. "They takes up nips and anglers, lodges 'em for a time in gaol, and then hangs 'em at Tyburn Gallows." He told her of the taverns, where she could find gentlemen with fat purses, and adult rogues who might aid her if she needed aid. Then he said, "I've saved it to the last—Saint Paul's Church. 'Tis where we nip today."

The kyncheon coves seemed very well known at the spireless church. The verger even nodded to them as they went into Duke Humphrey's Walk, the middle aisle of the church. No pious worshippers, Rosalind noticed, were praying here. Duke Humphrey's Walk was the rendezvous of all London. Friend met friend. Lawyers spoke with clients. Servants came to be hired. Lovers arrived and left arm in arm. Burdened, cursing porters struggled through the gossiping throngs while gallants flirted with women, who smiled at them over fluttering fans. Peddlers shouted their wares, and vendors hawked broadsides advertising that in Fleet Street for a "ha'penny ye can see monsters aplenty, six-fingered babies and two-headed calves." Saint Paul's was like no church Rosalind had dreamed could ever be. Londoners even used its font as a counter to pay money over. She was yet more horrified as she stood next to a large, square marble tomb watching Dickon and the other boy approach a fat man as their victim. The jostler, who Dickon called only Stall, fell hard against the fat man as if by accident, knocking him off balance against the tomb. While the small boy excused himself, Dickon ducked beside the man and, unseen, put his hand into the purse at his belt. Holding a coin high in silent triumph, Dickon motioned for Rosalind to leave the church with them as the fat man walked away, not knowing yet that he'd been robbed.

"On the morrow ye'll see me cut off a purse wi' my dagger," Dickon promised Rosalind. He looked beaming at her, but what he saw made his eyes grow sharp with sudden suspicion. "Ye've gone white as a dove. Ye have no stomach for nipping, eh?"

Sick to her stomach, Rosalind could only nod.

Dickon shook his head. "I seen four nips tucked up this year at Tyburn Gallows by the hangman. They had no stomach for it neither, so they were caught. I doubt ye'll make a nip, not ye, Rosalind, nor an angler nor even a clapperdudgeon." He spat into the foul-smelling drainage kennel in the center of the street. "The Upright Man should not a baptized ye. In two weeks' time ye'll still not be able ter cut a purse from a man's belt. 'Tis far more easy than nipping inter one. Yer hand may grow swift enough, but ye'll not put yer guts and will to it, I think."

III

THE GOLDSMITH'S GARDEN

Two weeks from that day Rosalind still was not able to take a coin from the purse without making the bells ring, nor could she angle with any skill. Dickon had been right in his prophecy.

That night she walked back to Moll's house from Smart's Quay in the summer rain behind Dickon and the jostler, her ears burning from their cruel comments about her lack of skill. As the rain dripped down her nose, she thought sadly of her grandfather and Cowley. She wished with all her heart that she were at home, thrashing or no thrashing, book or no book.

But as Moll had said, she could not get away. The kyncheon coves would not let her out of their sight. Dickon told her once, reading her thoughts, "If ye try to run from us, we'll cry for the City Watch and tell 'em ye prigged summat. They'll harken to us."

That day it also rained in County Sussex, south of London on the English Channel. The two men sat their horses at a crossroads. Adam Fenchurch spoke to his servant, "So, Martin, two old graybeards at long last are dead. Thanks to the Devil, you learned that the pastor in Cowley, my kinsman, died just ten days ago. And now at last my very noble kinsman, the Baron of Broome, is also dead. I've been too long in his house waiting for him to die." Fenchurch gestured toward the gray manor house below the hilltop crossroads. "Both men were very old. 'Tis not strange that they should die within days of one another."

"The girl lives yet, the pastor's grandchild, Master Fenchurch," remarked Martin Sclater.

"So she does, although we never would have known if you had not gone to Cowley and found the old man dead and newly buried. But the housekeeper says the girl ran away from Cowley."

"Aye, master. Still, by right, the pastor's grandchild is now the Lady Broome. She is the closest heir. You are next."

Fenchurch scowled at the rain-sodden ground. "She is. If she did not exist, I would be the Baron of Broome without question. No one here in Sussex knows of the existence of this girl. I told Lord Broome before he died only of his brother's death and of his brother's son's death in Spain— not one word of a great-niece. Before he died Lord Broome named me as his heir." He turned in his saddle to look questioningly at his serving man. "Martin, where do you think this girl has gone?"

"To London," answered the dark man after a moment's thought.

"I will claim the barony. But while she lives, I will never rest easy. Could you find her for me?"

Sclater nodded. "I think I could in time, master. Shall
I tell the girl that she has become a noble lady?"

Fenchurch shook his head, then laughed as he put the
hood of his cloak over his face against the downpour and
gathered up his reins. "No. Attend to it that my young
kinswoman never learns she is. You will stay in London
from now on. Come to me in Saint Albans when you have
found her. I must stay at Saint Albans until I've done my
business for the Queen's secretary. Martin, you learned in
Cowley something of the girl's appearance. It seems this
Rosalind resembles me somewhat from what you say. We
Broomes are often greatly like unto one another, fair-
haired with brown eyes. I saw the portrait of Lord Broome
when he was my age. You saw it also. This resemblance
should help you find my young kinswoman—even in London."

"Aye, master, it should." Martin bobbed his head as the
fingers of his right hand splayed out to touch the hilt of his
dagger.

For a full month Rosalind lived in Moll's house, trying
unsuccessfully day after day in the shed on Smart's Quay
to nip in silence. Before long only Moll would speak to her
in a kindly manner. Rosalind cherished her kindness and
the words said to her, though she knew Moll, too, was
aware that she would never be a good rogue. She knew
Moll wished her well. Where she'd been unwilling to serve
Lady Margaret, she served Moll, who had saved her from
the Abraham Man's rage. Rosalind found him constantly
on her mind, hoping he'd gone on his travels once more
and wondering if he'd sold Dr. Hornsby's book. His strange

words still puzzled her. One night while she brushed Moll's long hair, she asked, "My lady, who is the red witch Tom o' Bedlam speaks of?"

Moll laughed softly. "I am. Who else? Is not my hair red?"

Rosalind frowned, recalling the woman's speech to her at the Holy Lamb. There Moll had denied being a witch at all. No, she did not think Moll was Tom's red witch.

The next evening after that conversation Moll took Rosalind, Helen, the angler, and one of the boys aside. "There is a house in Blackfriars where one of us canting folk works as a kitchen maid. Go to the gate in the wall back of the house. She will let you in. It is not a lord's house, only a goldsmith's, but the goldsmith is rich. 'Tis said he has a cup made of an ostrich egg set in silver and gold he means to sell to a man at the Queen's court for a New Year's gift to the Queen. Bring me that cup, Helen. The Upright Man wants it. You, Ned," she addressed the boy, "bring me the purse of silver the merchant keeps under the pillow in his bedchamber, and you, Rosalind, bring me. . . ." She laughed. "Fetch me roses from the goldsmith's garden."

"When do we go, Moll?" asked Helen calmly.

"Tomorrow at eight of the clock. The goldsmith and his wife will not be at home. Tell the kitchen maid that you come from me."

"How will we know her?" asked Helen.

"Her name is Kate. Cry of lavender, Helen, and she will come to the gate. Her hair is fair as Rosalind's, but her face is marked by the smallpox. She may wear a scarlet petticoat."

"Will she give us saffron cakes?" asked the boy.

"No, there'll be no time for that. She'll give Helen a sack for the cup. The purse ye'll hide in your doublet, Ned. As for the roses, Rosalind can carry them as bold as if she'd paid out a ha'penny for them." Moll held up a finger. "Remember well, though. If someone cries 'thief' after ye and ye must run, do not come here to Whitefriars to my house. Lead the City Watch away. And if they catch ye, do not say ye know me or any other of the canting folk."

Rosalind sighed. Dickon had repeated this instruction over and over. It mattered not at all where the kyncheon coves ran, as long as it was not to Moll's house.

Later that evening small Ned came to sit next to Rosalind beside the kitchen fire. He said nothing but she knew by his stark paleness that he was as frightened as she. He was also new to Moll's house and had yet to steal. He said wistfully to Rosalind, "Tell me again of the tame dragons in Macedonia that eat eggs."

"The young dragons pierce an eggshell with their tails and suck the egg dry," explained the girl. "But apples are deadly poison to dragons. Did you know, Ned, that there are wild dogs in Ethiopia that have hands and feet like a man's?"

"Tell me of them." Ned slid close enough for Rosalind to notice that he was trembling.

As frightened as he, Rosalind thought that night again of escaping, but it wouldn't be possible. Dickon and the jostler slept on rushes at the top of the stairs. They slept very lightly. Anytime anyone opened a door in the night, one or the other called out, "Who's there?"

The house in Blackfriars was a fine timber one surrounded by a wall of stone. Helen, as the most experienced of the rogue children, took charge and led the way to the rear gate. There she called out, as if she were a street seller, "Lavender, lavender, bay, and rosemary. Lavender for your linens."

They waited. Rosalind's heart was in her mouth as she shifted from one foot to the other, hoping that no one would come to Helen's signal. But the gate opened soon, and a woman peered out. Her hair was covered by a white coif but her petticoat was scarlet.

"Ye'd be Kate?" asked Helen.

"Aye."

"We come from Moll."

"Ah." The maid opened the gate wider to permit the children to enter. The goldsmith's garden was a very fine one with lime and elm trees here and there, rosebushes aplenty, a herb garden, and paths made of crushed oyster shells. Kate led the way to the rear of the house, smiled, and lifted the latch of the kitchen door, motioning the three inside. Helen and Ned filed in, not Rosalind.

"Come, girl, make haste inside." The woman stamped her foot, frowning angrily at Rosalind.

"I was not bid to go inside. I came only for roses from the garden." Something in the woman's manner disturbed Rosalind. As the woman shut the door and pulled down the latch again, Rosalind backed away from her. She'd spied dark hair under the coif. And this woman was not pock-marked.

Suddenly she sprang at Rosalind, hands outstretched. Rosalind spun about and raced for the gate as the woman howled, "The girl, the girl is running away! Catch her!"

Rosalind ran through the gate, slamming it behind her
seconds before two men who had been waiting hidden beside the house reached it. While they got in each other's
way, clawing at the gate latch, Rosalind ran for her life.
She ran down the alleyway, her skirts hampering her speed.
Danger lay behind in the thudding footsteps of the men she
knew to be members of the City Watch. It had been a trap.
The woman had not been Kate, though she'd played Kate's
part. Helen and Ned were caught inside. And she would
have been, too, if Moll had not told her to get roses from
the garden.

Rosalind ran swiftly, turning and twisting down the narrow streets. She ran in front of a cart and behind it, knocking down an old man who cursed her. Dogs ran barking
after her, getting under her feet, making her stumble.
Shouts of "thief" came ringing after her. Suddenly ahead
of her she saw what might be her salvation, a puppet show,
surrounded by a throng of laughing watchers. She slowed
to a halt, edged in among them, and threaded her way to
the very front and stood panting while one puppet struck
the other over the head with a stick.

While she tried to catch her breath, the men of the
Watch passed by. But when she turned to go, she felt a
hand heavy on her arm. She looked up in horror into a
man's scowling face. Was he another of the Watch? But,
no, he was one of the canting men she'd seen her first day
in London, a finely dressed gallant, but a jackman, a forger
of documents. He hauled her out of the crowd.

"And where were ye bound just now?" he asked her.
"I saw ye come. I saw the Watch after ye."

She answered without thinking. No rogue would harm

her. "To Whitefriars." Then she clapped a hand over her mouth. Moll's house was the last place in London she was to run to. And she had been going toward it when she saw the puppet show!

The forger said, "As I thought—to Moll's house. This is a matter for the Upright Man." He took tight hold of her arm. "You and I will go to the Gun in Billingsgate. I've just come from there. Ye'll find him there and Moll besides." He shook her slightly. "They will judge ye."

"The Abraham Man? Is he there, too?"

"Aye, Tom o' Bedlam is." The forger pulled her away with him. She was too full of fear to resist his grasp.

In fish-smelling Billingsgate Rosalind saw the rogues assembled, Moll sitting again beside the Upright Man. Tom o' Bedlam, once more in his rags, sat at a nearby table.

The Upright Man shouted the moment he saw her and the forger, "Where is the goldsmith's cup?"

Rosalind trembled so her knees shook together. "Please sir, the Watch caught Ned and Helen. It was a snare." She spoke to Moll. "My lady, it was not Kate who let us in. It was another woman with dark hair."

The forger announced, "This girl was making for Whitefriars."

"Were ye?" asked Moll.

"Aye, my lady, I was too much afraid to remember."

The Upright Man turned to his sweetheart. "Ye said she will never be a nip or angler. What use then will we have from her? The men of the Watch have seen her face. What shall we do with her?"

"Rid ourselves of her," growled Tom o' Bedlam. "Strangle her as I'd strangle a cat that clawed me."

"Aye," agreed another rogue. "The girl will fail ye agin, Moll, and will lead the Watch to ye next time."

Tom o' Bedlam drank more ale. "Strangle her. Send her to the river." He got up from his bench.

Moll arose at the same instant. "Rosalind is my matter, Tom, not yours. 'Tis no fault of hers that Helen and Ned will be hanged at Tyburn Gallows."

"Is it not? Did she lure the Watch by her mouth or her actions? Does she tell ye the truth, Moll?"

"I tell you the truth!" Rosalind cried, as the man came out from behind the table.

And then she saw the silvery flashing of a blade as the Upright Man's dagger flew in front of her to thud into the wood of the table before Tom. Moll had thrown it with good aim.

"The girl is a rogue!" the woman cried. "She has been baptized by us. It is true she has no stomach for our business. She would be caught the second time and hang. Let her go. Rosalind will not tell the Watch of us. She will keep her clapper silent. I'll vouch for her."

There was quiet for a time. Then a prigger of prauncers spoke up. "Upright Man, is this a matter for the Devil?"

"No. He has far greater matters to occupy him at the moment." He waved his hand. "I say Moll shall have her way."

The woman smiled at Rosalind as Tom sat down, mumbling angrily. She spoke to a young rogue, "Giles, go to my house and fetch me the clothing this girl wore when she first came to London." Moll took off her shears and clicked the blades together. "What do ye say? Shall she lose her hair or lose her life?"

The Upright Man grabbed Moll around her waist,

kissed her, let her go, and cried, "Clever ye are to trick the Watch so, Moll!"

Moll spoke to Rosalind. "Ye came to London as a lad. Ye will go from London as one. The Watch hunt for a girl. They'll find no girl. Now go to the kitchen here and wait for me to bring your clothing."

An hour later Moll's work was done. Rosalind wore her father's boyhood garments again, and lengths of her long yellow hair lay atop the rubbish heap in the corner of the Gun's kitchen. When Moll had finished, Rosalind felt her head with both hands. How cold her head was. How very strange it felt.

The woman told her, "Ye make a pretty lad. All the girls will want to kiss ye." She held open the kitchen door. "Do not come back to my house, but if ye have great need of us, come to this tavern or the Holy Lamb. We baptized ye. Ye have still a claim on us, I say. Where will ye go now?"

"Home to Cowley, my lady. I'll be beaten very hard, for losing the book and for seeing the play. But I will go home."

Moll started to laugh. "Stay a day in London then. See other plays. Your grandfather cannot beat you more for seeing two or three plays than for seeing one."

"No, he cannot, my lady." Rosalind curtseyed to her.

"No, no!" Moll cried. "Bow to a lady. Remember you are Robin Broome until you are at home again. You must bear yourself as a lad. Do you remember the roads home?"

"Yes."

"Then go first to the playhouse. After that, go home, but strive to remember me."

"I will not forget you, my lady. I owe my life to you."

"And I will never forget the girl who called me 'my lady,' though I am only Moll Cutpurse. Beware of Tom o' Bedlam."

"I shall, my lady." And Rosalind slipped out of the Gun into the street, free again. Even the air of Billingsgate, where all London came to buy fish, smelled of perfume to her.

She set off to Holywell Fields, where she knew two theaters lay. There was to be a play today. She had read the playbills posted at the north end of London Bridge. She had not dared asked the Upright Man or Moll for money, and she had very little. The fee to see a play was a penny in London Town as well as in Oxford. Rosalind had but two farthings. But even if she could not go inside, she could take comfort in seeing a *real* theater, not a country innyard. Perhaps a second miracle would occur? Being released by the canting men was one miracle already today. She could hope for another, couldn't she?

From Billingsgate it was a long walk to Holywell Fields outside London. Rosalind was footsore by the time she left Shoreditch Road and walked across the green field to the Curtain, a high, round building with an enclosed outside staircase. North of it she saw the second wooden playhouse, the one Londoners named the Theatre. It looked much the same as the Curtain. A flag signaling that a play was to be shown that day flapped above the Curtain.

By the time Rosalind arrived it was near one o'clock. The playgoers were gathering. Young oath-swearing gallants pushed by her outside the Curtain without so much as a by-your-leave. Many poorer citizens, judging by their somber garb, also came to the play. Some of them she knew by their blue doublets and flat caps to be London apprentices, no older than she. She envied them their pennies, as they shouldered past her to pay the gatherer at the door and go through her turnstile. Rich folk, too, arrived. Rosalind now marked out the nip and jostler hunting victims and shrank back into the moving throng, so she would not be seen by them. She did not want to watch them at their work either.

At last she stood alone in front of the playhouse. No second miracle had taken place to afford her a penny to enter. She had not truly expected one, she told herself. It had been wishful thinking.

But at least she could listen. She could hear the noisy hum of the excited crowd. All at once she heard a trumpet sounded with a flourish. Envious, she went on telling herself she would start for Cowley in another moment. But she knew from the play she'd seen in Oxford that there would be three tuckets of the trumpet before the play began. Why not stay to hear the trumpet? That cost nothing.

As the hard, round, golden note of the second trumpet blast faded from her hearing, she heard another sound, the quick thud of hooves. Riders galloped along Shoreditch Road. As she turned to look toward the sound, she saw them coming—four men mounted on Barbary horses, three chestnuts and a great black.

How richly garbed were the young men, who reined in not far from her, in velvet cloaks and plumed court bonnets. Rosalind saw the tall man astride the rearing black look about him, laughing. He stared at Rosalind, alone in the meadow, smiled at her, and called out to his companions, "We may be behind time today, my lords, but all the same I seem to have some luck. I've found us a pretty boy to hold our horses for two shillings, have I not, boy?"

Two shillings! Rosalind bowed very low, wishing she had a fine cap to doff. "Yes, my lord."

"Ah, the boy's not London-bred. Not with such good manners." In one easy movement the man was off his horse.

The other three, all younger than the first, also dismounted and gave their reins to Rosalind. Not one spoke to her. She saw only flashes of silken splendor under the cloaks of two of the bejeweled youths, but the third paused beside the older man, who fished two shilling silver pieces out of his purse and gave them to Rosalind. The third man was handsome, his hair long and golden with a red rose tied to one lock.

"You did not tell me. What is the play today?" the older, fair-haired man asked the youth with the rose.

"'Tis called *The Taming of the Shrew*. Not a new play but a good one."

"Well, then, we shall see it," came from the first lord, who turned and strode toward the Curtain with the others.

Astonished and wondering, now that she had charge of four horses, how she was to see the play, Rosalind stood gawking after the four lords. When they had gone inside the playhouse, she gave her attention to the horses. She marveled at their velvet upholstered saddles and the silver on their bridles, then stared down at the silver in her hand. How astonishing. They had paid her before she had done the work for them. A miracle indeed. This seemed a day of them.

While she stood amazed, Dickon and the jostler came running up to her. They had been behind the playhouse hoping to find a way to sneak up the staircase, but had found none. And they had had no success nipping either. If they had got two pennies, they would have gone into the Curtain to ply their trade there.

Dickon said to her, "We know ye, Rosalind, though yer head's been shorn. Who did it? I see ye've found yer trade at last. A horse thief. Ye be a good prigger of prauncers."

Before Rosalind could find her tongue to tell Dickon what astonishing things had happened to her that day, the jostler spoke up, "Na, Dickon. Look ter the black prauncer. Ye was yet behind the playhouse when the great lords come ridin', but I seen 'em. 'Twas the Lord Essex, hisself, who give the black prauncer ter Rosalind to hold. Essex, hisself, the Queen's favorite."

IV
THE PLAYERS

"Essex?" exclaimed Rosalind in disbelief.

The jostler nodded. "An' the young man wi' the red posy in his hair was the Earl o' Southampton. Him we jostled once in the Strand. 'Twas a fine rich purse we got off him. They all be great lords."

Rosalind was astonished. A third miracle. Her fondest dream had come true. She had seen the man her father had sailed to Spain with, the Earl of Essex, the greatest man in England. What would her grandfather say to that?

Dickon interrupted her thoughts. "What do ye here? Who shore yer head?"

Rosalind sighed. The third trumpet blast had blown some time past, yet here she was holding horses—though somewhat richer. "Moll did." She explained swiftly to the two boys what had happened at the goldsmith's house.

Dickon looked somber, then said, "'Tis my guess the Watch got Kate too before they set the snare. She musta told 'em of it. She'll hang with Ned and Helen."

"Aye," Rosalind agreed unhappily. She told the boys,

"I'm going home today but first I wished to see a play."
She laughed. "But at least I've seen a playhouse."

Dickon shrugged. "Go inside. We'll hold the prauncers
for ye. Ye can leave the playhouse afore the lords do.
They'll never be the wiser."

Tempted, Rosalind hesitated, then said, "You'd prig
them, Dickon."

The nip's honor as a rogue was threatened, and he
growled at her, "Na. Wasn' ye baptized one o' us by the
Upright Man? What's more, all London Town knows the
Earl of Essex's black horse. 'Twas a gift the old Queen
gave him. Who'd buy that horse 'o me? He'd be hanged
with me."

For a few moments Rosalind gazed in doubt over the
fields. Then, hearing a cheer, she surrendered the reins,
ran to the door of the Curtain, and paid one of the earl's
shillings to the grumbling woman gatherer, who counted
out eleven pennies to her.

The play was about to start. A tall man was speaking a
witty welcome to the audience, as Rosalind grabbed her
pennies and pushed her impatient way in among the people standing below the stage. While she listened to the
player's fine flow of words and watched his gestures, she
stared about her. Aye, the Curtain was far finer than the
innyard of the White Swan. Here a permanent stage had
been built at one end of the roofless theater open to the
clear, warm summer sky. On three sides a platform pro-
jected out over the audience standing below it. The fourth
side of the platform-stage was built into the playhouse wall.
At its top, protruding into the open air, she saw a hutlike
structure. Below this was a sort of gallery supported on ten-

foot-high columns between green silk hangings. There musicians sat with their drums, tabors, and viols. At the very back of the stage were two doors, leading where she did not know. The stage on which the welcoming player stood in his long black gown was draped about its sides and front with scarlet cloth. Young men, members of the audience, sat on stools on each side of the stage, smoking pipes, eating apples, and basking in the admiration of the crowd.

The player speaking the welcome went on, giving Rosalind time to look away from the stage into the circular galleries to her left, right, and behind her. She saw three galleries, one above the other, filled with the more prosperous Londoners, who sat on cushions and benches. In a gallery to her right she spied Essex and the young lords. He laughed and talked with his companions and nodded to all who bowed or curtseyed to him, though they be rich and important folk or humble men in the pit where she stood. But when she saw his eyes ranging over the people below him, she ducked behind a tall Londoner for fear she might be recognized as the "pretty boy" who was supposed to be outside holding horses.

Then the play began, and Rosalind forgot her fears of being marked out by the nobleman. Once more she was lost in the fairy world she had entered in Oxford. She was not in England at all but in far-off Italy. She became parcel and part of the lively play, enraptured by the beauty of the costumes and of the wonderful words.

With the other common playgoers, the groundlings, Rosalind laughed till tears came to her eyes at the clever sallies and tricks of the man who tried to tame the fiery

Katherina and who finally succeeded in turning her into a gentle lady. She heard out the very last words of the play, but when four of the players came forward dancing, jigging comically across the stage to suit the final speech, she recalled the nip and the horses. Hiding behind groundlings, she slipped through the audience to the outside. What if the nip hadn't kept his word? What if he'd run off with the horses? Cold with terror, she looked about her, then sighed with relief. Aye, there were the horses, still held by the small rogues. She ran to them, took the reins, and gave pennies to the nip and jostler. She watched them dart off to station themselves outside the playhouse, hoping for rich prey to pass them.

Moments later the flushed-faced crowd came boiling out of the Curtain and down Shoreditch Road. Rosalind waited, soothing the horses, as they caught the excitement of the people and snorted and moved about. Last of all came the Earl of Essex and his friends. The four lords did not walk alone. Three others walked with them. One of them was a boy near Rosalind's own age.

In front of the great earl Rosalind was tongue-tied. She wanted to tell him of her father but could not find the words. She could only steady the black horse as best she could, look wistfully at the man, and hope for another word from him. She did not get it.

Instead, she heard the words of one of the newcomers. He was a short, rather heavy man with a handsome head, large dark eyes, very dark beard, and a warm pleasant voice. Somehow his voice was familiar, though Rosalind knew she had never seen him before. "Fare you well, my lord," he told Essex. "I am honored that you came today to our poor play."

"Master Burbage, I think I fancy your kings better than your lover in today's play, though you played the tamer of the shrew very well."

Then the earl spoke to the largest of the three newcomers. This man was red-faced, blue-eyed, and the possessor of the thickest, longest, forked beard Rosalind had ever seen. "Master Pope, tell Master Shakespeare for me that I was again very well pleased by a play of his."

Pope could bow very low for a man his size, Rosalind thought. He said, "Indeed, my lord, I shall tell Master Will. He will be greatly pleased."

Rosalind had expected Essex to mount his horse, but instead he clapped the boy standing next to Pope on the shoulder. Then he peered behind him very closely and with his finger touched the boy back of his right ear. The earl laughed, holding up his whitened finger so all could see it. He hooted, "Young Master Gulliford has the whiteness of the sweet lady Katherina's neck upon him still."

The golden-haired gray-eyed boy smiled up at the earl. "I hoped you liked me today, my lord."

Essex pulled himself onto his horse, taking the reins from Rosalind. The other lords followed suit. Moments later they waved to the actors but not to Rosalind.

She stood bowing with them as the lords rode off at a hard gallop, forcing the slow-moving, walking Londoners to the sides of the road. Rosalind heard their cheers as Essex passed by. The two adult players, Burbage and Pope, started back at once to the playhouse, arguing about something as they went. The boy, Gulliford, stood near her, still gazing after the noblemen and frowning. Rosalind stared hard at him as Essex had done. Aye, there was a streak of white paint behind his ear. This lad had played the pretty Katherina, the heroine of the play she'd just seen. "Master Gulliford" Essex had called him, and Gulliford's garments were those of a boy—doublet, breeches, and hose. But then so were hers!

Where she had been shy of the men players and the lords, she was not shy of the boy. When he started for the Curtain, she ran after him. "Were you truly the lady of the play?"

The boy nodded, laughing. "I was truly Katherina as I have been Titania, the fairy queen. When I was small, I was Puck, the goblin." Master Gulliford had changed his voice now, making it sweeter and higher. Yes, Rosalind recognized it as the very voice of the fierce shrew girl in today's play.

"Who would you be?" Gulliford asked.

"Robin Broome of Cowley, in Oxfordshire." As she hurried along beside him, a mad idea, one which came out of nowhere at all, struck her. She gestured toward the Curtain. "Could I find work there?"

The boy stopped in his tracks, eyed her up and down, and asked, "What can you do? Are you a player of some country company? No, you are not. If so, you would not have asked me if boys play women's parts."

Rosalind shook her head. "I am no player at all, Master Gulliford," she told him. "When I have a man's height I want to be a soldier, but I think my grandfather has hopes of making a pastor of me, too."

To her surprise, the handsome boy started to chuckle. "So did my grandsire!" he said. "How very strange. A pastor. It must be a thing old men do. I ran away from home to my Uncle Condell because he was a player, and I had wished to be one since I saw my first play. I like being a player, but I do not like my Uncle Condell. So you have run away, too?"

"I did not say that I had run away."

He laughed. "I know you have." Then he did a strange thing. Exactly as if he had known Rosalind for years, he linked his arm with hers, dragging her along with him. He was far stronger than he looked. "You come with me, Robin. Because you have also suffered from pastors, I'll take you in my favor. I'll take you to my dear Uncle Condell and the other players. Perhaps they will have a use for you. We are not all players at the Curtain. Other folk do lesser things. If Master Burbage or my good uncle have no use for you, I know an apple seller who might have you help her sell her apples among the penny stinkards."

"What are they, Master Gulliford?"

The boy snorted in contempt. "The groundlings, the common folk, who stand below the stage."

Rosalind did not tell him she had been a humble groundling that day. Gulliford took her through a door at the rear marked *For Players Only*. They climbed some steps inside, opened a second door, and to Rosalind's great amazement were suddenly in a forest. Six tall bay trees blocked her way. Under one tree lay a man's severed bloody head. She stopped dead before it, covering her mouth so she wouldn't cry out.

Gulliford laughed and kicked the head away with his foot, making it roll along under the trees. "That is only the earl's head. It is not real. We use it for a play. You are among our properties, Robin." He pointed to a king's jeweled scepter on a table, lying next to a set of well-feathered wings. Nearby stood a small bush covered with gilded wooden apples. Beside it was a huge bed of state with an altar at its foot and next to that some painted shields stacked against a mossy green bank. Other properties strewn about were far too strange for Rosalind to try to guess what they might be.

Gulliford took her past the properties to a wide space behind the stage, the tiring room, where a group of men and boys stood around a long table littered with rolls of paper and pots of paints and ointments. Some of the players were still in their wigs and costumes for *The Taming of the Shrew,* waiting their turns for the tiring men to help them disrobe. But most were in everyday garments, all puffed, padded, and slashed, and of most fashionable colors. To Rosalind's eyes the players seemed to be as great lords as Essex and his friends were. Certainly they were garbed near as dazzling.

Rosalind, the boy actor with her, and the other players stood quiet to hear Richard Burbage saying, "Then it is agreed? We shall take ourselves across the Thames to Southwark?"

"Aye, Richard," came Thomas Pope's rich deep voice. The heavy-set player Rosalind had seen outside the playhouse looked at the man seated next to him. "What say you to this, Master Will?"

Master Will, Rosalind saw, was pale with lustrous dark eyes and graying, receding dark hair. His forehead was abnormally high, his brows dark and arched, his nose long, and his mouth full and red. His white ruff was small and discreet, his doublet, hose, and breeches all of black silk. Where others of the company of players were gaudy birds,

this man was a somber raven. But somehow in his white
and black he was more to be noticed than they. Master
Will answered Pope, "I say we should take ourselves across
the Thames. I have found Southwark to my liking."

Burbage nodded. "As all of you know, the other playhouse in these fields, the Theatre, belongs to my family.
The landlord owns the ground beneath it but not the wood
it is made of. Aye, we shall take down my Theatre. I can
do nothing to force the landlord here in Holywell Fields to
see reason and renew my lease. So we shall pull down the
timbers and build a new playhouse out of them across the
Thames. Until that is done, we shall remain here playing
at the Curtain and at our private playhouse in Blackfriars."

"Aye, so we shall," said another player, a dignified
youngish man with a long clever face.

Gulliford jabbed Rosalind in the side with his elbow.
"That is Henry Condell, my uncle and my master. I live
with him and his shrew wife and let him take my wages. I
could gain more favor and have more money elsewhere.
I need no master now."

Rosalind was not much interested in Gulliford's affairs.
She pointed to Burbage and whispered to the boy, "What
are they talking of?"

Gulliford sighed. "The Burbage family own both playhouses here in Holywell Fields, the Curtain and the Theatre. They are talking about moving the Theatre to Southwark over the river. Why don't you listen well?"

Rosalind could not believe her ears, even though twice
she had heard this talk. Move an entire building as enormous as a playhouse! That would be a chore indeed. What
manner of odd folk were these players to speak so calmly

of such a tremendous undertaking. "Is everyone I see here a player?" she asked Gulliford.

"Aye, near every man now—even Master Will—though he is better suited to write plays, I think, than to play in them."

Burbage clapped his hands together to get everyone's attention. "Then it is agreed. Do not prattle of this matter in London. I do not want our landlord to hear of it. Before long we shall dismantle the Theatre in secret. But tonight we meet here again to rehearse the play the Queen's Master of Revels has chosen to commence the days of Christmas at Whitehall Palace. Each of you should have his cue sheet by now."

The players moved off, murmuring and nodding. Those garbed to go into London walked toward the rear door. Those yet in costume went to the tiring men, who had waited at a distance to remove wigs, paint, and gowns. Soon only Pope, Burbage, Condell, and Master Will remained behind. Gulliford tugged Rosalind by the sleeve up to them. She bowed, remembering her manners and Moll's warning.

"Bones o' God," said Condell wearily. "Who is this boy, Nephew?"

"Robin Broome, Uncle. He seeks employment here."

"What do you do?" asked Burbage, eyeing Rosalind as if he measured her like an inchworm. "Do you sing? Can you bear a part in a song?"

"No, sir. I do not sing well." Rosalind found fierce-eyed Burbage terrifying. She found all of them terrifying except for Gulliford.

"Are you a player from some country company?" asked

Burbage. "Your face is not uncomely, and you are well made and not too tall as yet."

"No, sir."

"But I think you want to be a player, do you not?" The gentle question came from Master Will, who was smiling.

Rosalind was silent for a long moment. So many strange things had taken place that day that her head was spinning. She could not say that she did not want to be a player, for that would insult the players. "I think I would like to be a player, yes," she found herself saying.

Burbage grunted. "Do you play the flute or viol? Can you dance?"

Rosalind first shook her head, then nodded it. "I do not play the flute or viol, sir, but I can dance."

"Dance for us then, my boy," commanded Thomas Pope. He, too, had a smile for her where Burbage and Condell had none.

Without music, without even her own whistling, and afraid to sing, Rosalind began a morris dance. She did her best, trying to imagine that her knees were tied with morris bells and she had a tabor player beside her. As she pranced about the tiring room, she knew that the dance she had done along the Cowley road had been the better one, the happy morris before she fell in with Tom o' Bedlam.

No player commented on her dance when Burbage shouted, "Enough!" Yet she had seen both Pope and Master Will smile again as she had capered near them.

"How old are you, lad?" asked Burbage.

"Thirteen years, come Candlemas next."

Pope raised a bushy eyebrow. "A very likely age, twelve years, Master Burbage."

Condell put in sourly, "I say this lad has too little knack for it, and he is too old to be trained thoroughly. I had Gulliford come to me at ten, and I took Davey, my other lad, when he was but eight years. I have need of a servant at my house in Saint Mary Aldermansbury. We have lads enough here at the playhouse for the poor kind of work this boy could do."

"Come to think upon it, Master Condell, I have need of a servant also," volunteered Thomas Pope. Leaning against the table, his arms folded, he spoke to Rosalind. "Which of us do you choose for a master? Condell here in London Town or myself across the Thames in Southwark?"

Rosalind looked from one player to the other in dismay. While she had danced, she had thought more about being a player. It would be wondrous exciting to play a part at the Curtain. She could perform a time or two, then go home to Cowley later. She would have a longer holiday and an interesting one in London Town as a player. A thrashing would still await her in Cowley, of course, but why not be hanged for a sheep as for a lamb? She could be a player lad for a time. Why not? No one seemed to guess that she was no lad at all.

But to be a servant to a player? That was another matter indeed. Should she refuse them both as she had refused to serve Lady Margaret? But if she refused, she must go from London at once. The money she had would take her home but not permit her to stay unless she found other employment. She looked at Condell, then at Pope. The big player had smiled at her while she danced.

She liked Pope better. Another point in his favor was that he did not live in London. She would not be so likely to see Tom o' Bedlam in Southwark as in the city. And the

Watch of Southwark would not be made up of the same men as the Watch in London. What was more she had never been to Southwark. Dickon and the jostler had never crossed London Bridge with her. They had plied their trade only in the city. Southwark had its own rogues.

Rosalind bowed to Pope. "I will serve you, Master Pope."

Burbage laughed and addressed Pope. "Ah, Thomas, your fame goes before you with a trumpet calling your name. This boy knows it. We have not once said it here."

Rosalind put in, "I heard the lords speak your name when I held their horses for them today."

Master Will chuckled. "Here's an honest lad, Thomas. Treat him kindly. He will never flatter your player's vanity." To Rosalind directly, the playwright said, "That is how I began to make my fortune, also, by holding gentlemen's horses outside a playhouse. I was then far older than you are." As he got up and walked with Burbage out onto the stage, Rosalind noticed that Master Will limped, though slightly.

Their departure left only Condell and Pope behind at the table. Condell spoke to Gulliford before he turned to follow Shakespeare and Burbage. "Do not be late tonight to rehearsal, John."

"No, Uncle." Gulliford waited until Condell was out of earshot, then in front of Pope said boldly, "You did well, Robin, in choosing Tom Pope here. Mistress Gillet is the best cook in all of Southwark."

"Who is Mistress Gillet? asked Rosalind.

Pope had a warm, deep laugh. "Dame Gillet Willingson keeps my house. I am a bachelor. Come home with me now, and I will show you to her. I will fetch my cloak, and we shall go." As the old player moved heavily to the far corner of the tiring room, Gulliford tugged at Rosalind's arm. "I had feared you would choose my uncle. You will have a fine master in Tom Pope. He is kindly. So is Master Will. The others are not always so sweet-tempered. Hear me well, Robin. Master Pope has had many lads live with him and Dame Gillet. Some of them are players now. He will bring you here often with him to the playhouse if you carry yourself cleverly and serve him well. He likes you. Perhaps he will make a player of you as Condell did of me. You are not yet too old. Players take apprentices, too. Boy players are paid half the wages of a man."

Rosalind gazed ruefully across the tiring room at another boy player, who had also acted the part of a lady in the play that day. He was wigless now and being helped out of his woman's silken bodice. "Must I play a maiden if I am to be a player?" It seemed past belief to her that she, a girl, pretending to be a boy, would act women's parts. Why not the parts of boys? She had had enough of skirts, hampering things that they were.

Gulliford laughed at her unhappy expression. "Come now, Robin, you are too tall to play a child or a fairy and too young and short to play a man. Most of this company played only women's parts when they were young. It will not disgrace you."

Rosalind did not say the words in the back of her mind. To be a player would disgrace her grandfather. If she should ever become a player, she would have to keep this fact as secret from him as her month among the canting men. What story should she tell him to explain her long absence when she returned home? She did not know.

Her arms around her master's thick waist, Rosalind rode

on horseback down Shoreditch Road. When they had left the Curtain behind them, Pope asked, "Do you think you have made a bad bargain in choosing to be my servant?"

She was truthful. "I would rather be a player, Master Pope."

The man grunted as his horse stumbled in a rut. Then he asked, "Do you read and write?"

"Aye, sir. I read English, Latin, and some Greek."

Pope chuckled. Rosalind thought he sounded pleased. "Perhaps, Robin Broome, you are too much of a scholar for me. I have very little Latin and no Greek at all. Tell of yourself."

Choosing her words very carefully, Rosalind told him of her pastor grandfather in Oxfordshire and of the valuable book the vagabond had stolen. Lying somewhat, she told him of her trip to London pursuing the thief. Not one word did she speak of her weeks with the rogues or of her grandfather's anger with her, and most certainly she did not say that she was not a lad. She finished with, "I still seek the thief. You will not write my grandfather that I am here, Master Pope?"

"That is for you to do, Robin. And I do not think a pastor would be honored to hear from a 'godless player,' which is what most clergy call us." Pope asked a sudden hard question. "Robin, are you of gentle birth?"

Off guard, Rosalind spoke before she had thought out her answer. "Aye, Master Pope, I am." She went on more carefully. "My grandfather tells me we Broomes are of gentle birth, for all that we are very poor. I have never seen my kin in Sussex, and my grandfather misliked them." Aye, let Master Pope think she was of gentle birth but not that she was nobly born. Between a gentleman and a lord lay a monstrous gulf, one she, Rosalind Broome, could never cross. Let it suffice that she was gentle-born. She doubted that the old player would believe the truth, which she only half believed herself.

"I had guessed by your manner that you were," said Pope. "Why is it that you are willing to be my servant? Is it to live among players?"

"Yes, master." As they jogged along in silence, Rosalind had a happy idea come to her. She would save her pay and at the bookstalls in Saint Paul's Churchyard buy another copy of the book Tom o' Bedlam had stolen from her. When she had the book, she would go back to Cowley. That would ease her grandfather's wrath somewhat.

"Robin, I claim gentle birth myself," murmured the old actor. He went on, "To be wellborn and become a servant is not a fit thing. Perhaps I will find myself another serving lad so you can attend me at the playhouse."

"What could I do there for you, master?" Rosalind did not try to keep the joy from her voice. She'd been afraid she would scour dirty pots in Pope's kitchen.

"You will fill my pipe for me and help me into my boots. You will make yourself useful. Would you like that?"

"Yes, master, I want to see the plays—all of them."

"What plays have you seen?"

"Only today's play and one in Oxfordshire." She told him the plot of the play she'd seen.

"Yes, I have played a part or two in that. I play large clowns. It is an old play but a very good one." Pope was chuckling again as his horse trotted down Fish Street toward gloomy, many-arched London Bridge. He said, "Tonight Dame Gillet is to serve me whiting with galantine sauce, hen with leeks, and almond tarts. I seldom dine before I play a part, so I have a good stomach for my supper. Does my poor player's fare suit you, Robin?"

Rosalind closed her eyes in delight, envisioning these magnificent dishes she had never tasted. Most of her life she had eaten herring, bread and cheese, and porridge. Dame Gillet must be a praiseworthy cook, indeed. She said, "I do not think the Queen herself sups better tonight, Master Pope."

"I do not think she does at that." He sighed. "Her mind can never rest easy, Robin. She must always fear to lose her throne. And she is old, older than I. I doubt that she eats with a good appetite. She. . . ."

Intent upon the player's comment about Queen Elizabeth, Rosalind took no notice at all of the dark-faced man who had come over the bridge from Southwark. He guided his horse at a walk north along Fish Street on the opposite side from Pope and Rosalind. His darting eyes scrutinized the faces of the folk streaming out of Southwark as if he searched for someone in particular. He looked hardest at the girls and young women who walked toward the dark shadows of the bridge. He aimed a black-eyed glance at the odd pair, the cloaked elderly man and the fair-haired boy who passed him riding double on the gray horse. For an instant it seemed to him that the boy had a familiar look. But, no, this was a boy.

Martin Sclater sought a girl, not a lad. He scowled as he rode into London. Another day was passing, and he had not found Rosalind Broome. Adam Fenchurch was not a patient man!

V

COPYIST

The famous bells of Saint Saviour's Church greeted Rosalind as she and Thomas Pope rode westward along the south bank of the Thames past the brick palace of the Bishop of Winchester and down several of Southwark's meandering streets. She judged from the many red lattices she saw that they traveled streets of taverns. "Do men drink much wine and ale here, Master Pope?"

"Oh, lad, they do. Southwark is not a place of good reputation according to the sour folk who preach in London, but Dame Willingson and I like it well enough, for all that there are five prisons here. May you never see one of them from the wrong side of their gates, Robin. They are very terrible."

The actor's horse chose its wary way across a plank set over a ditch. Southwark, Rosalind noticed, was a place of swamps, criss-crossed with ditches and small bridges. She looked westward across the marshes to where she saw some tall wooden buildings much like the Curtain and the Theater. "Master Pope, is one of those the Bear Garden?" She'd heard of it from Dickon.

"Aye, lad, the other is a playhouse belonging to the Lord Admiral's Men, our rivals. We are the Lord Chamberlain's Men, you know. As for the Bear Garden, you would scent the stink of the bears and bulls if this were a warm day. Be glad that it is not."

They came to the end of a street and stopped before a house finer by far than Moll's in Whitefriars. Thomas Pope, for all of his talk about being a "poor player," was no poor man. His three-storied house even boasted a carved front. On each side of the house were gardens with tall limes rearing their green limbs above neat brick walls. Pope dismounted and handed his reins to a little lad who seemingly materialized out of the earth. Rosalind, too, slid down.

"Come," ordered the player, as the boy took the horse behind the house through a gate. "I will take you to Mistress Willingson. She will not find a pastor's grandson unseemly. You will know your catechism, and that will please her."

Like all London houses, Pope's was narrow with a pantry, buttery, and kitchen on the ground floor. Unlike Moll's, the air was fragrant here. Rosalind scented sweet herbs as the player shouted, "Dame Gillet! Dame!"

A woman came slowly down the dark hallway with a pan of burning herbs in her hands. She curtseyed to Pope, the pan held out before her, smoking, and gazed at Rosalind. Mistress Willingson was a handsome woman with dark hair, pulled back under a caul of gold and black wires. Her eyes were large and dark and her face white, but not painted as Rosalind had noticed those of so many London ladies were. Her clothing was good, a kirtle of milk-and-water blue, a black lawn apron, and a bodice of the same pale blue as her skirt. She said, "I try to ward off the plague with sweet herbs, Master Pope." She gestured with the herb pan. Then she asked him, "Who, pray, is this? Another player lad?" It seemed to Rosalind that she spoke as if Pope fetched home strange lads every day of the week. The woman went on, "This one does not have the look of a rogue about him, but I would say he has the evil smell of Whitefriars. He will be bathed first. Then he will be fed."

Suddenly frightened of the prospect of a bath, Rosalind blurted, "I do not need to be bathed."

"You do, indeed," said Mistress Willingson.

"No!" Rosalind felt the blood rising to her face. What if Master Pope or Dame Gillet were with her while she bathed? She started for the open door, but Pope caught her by the arm.

She heard his roar of laughter. "Dame, see how he can blush. He will have no need for paint if he ever plays a shy maiden's part. See to it that he bathes in private. He is of gentle birth, reads Latin and Greek, and is the grandson of a pastor."

"All the same a ball of sweet soap would not be amiss for him." The woman smiled and motioned for Rosalind to follow her. Clearly Mistress Willingson's approval was important to Pope. Rosalind wondered as she followed behind the thin, perfumed trail of herb and smoke, embarrassed by her "evil smell," how many lads the old actor had brought home to be bathed. How many had stayed servants to him? How many had become players?

Rosalind splashed in the dim kitchen before the warmth of the large brick oven in a deep wooden tub with a ball of scented soap. While she spluttered, washing her head,

Dame Gillet came in, threw a large towel at her, and left, saying, "Put this about you and call me, shy Robin, when you are clean. Do not forget to wash your ears and neck."

When she was wrapped in the towel, Rosalind cried out "Dame" and Mistress Willingson came in with clothing for her. There was a blue doublet, blue breeches and hose, and a small ruff, all somewhat worn, Rosalind noted, as she donned them after the woman had gone out again. But they were clean and they fit her well enough. The sight of them pleased her. They were a good omen. If she was to be a servant, she was not to be a common one. Common servants wore canvas doublets, not good woolen ones, and certainly not fashionably padded doublets like this one.

As Dame Gillet later yanked a comb through her wet hair, she said, "You will sup with the stable lad, the servingman, and the maids in the kitchen. You will sleep in the attic. I have chars for you to do for me in the morning. You will go shopping with me and carry my basket."

Pope came into the kitchen at that moment, puffing on his pipe. "No, dame, Robin will have the chamber the last lad slept in. Robin goes back to the Curtain with me tonight."

"Hah! Little use I shall have of him then. I mark your game. Another son, Master Pope? Yet *another*?" Dame Gillet sighed.

Rosalind supped that evening far more grandly than ever before. The food was marvelous and came not from wooden trenchers but from heavy pewter dishes. The two young maids piled her plate high and vowed she ate as heartily as the brawny young servingman. Then they sent her climbing through the well-furnished house to inspect the bedchamber on the third floor. To her way of thinking, the "last lad" in this house had been no servant. Had he been a player? This chamber was better than hers in Cowley. It had a featherbed and a walnut bedstead with blue canopy and hangings, a table and brass ewer, and, to her utter astonishment, a looking glass. She had never seen such a wondrous thing before. She spent long moments gazing by candlelight at her clean face. Yes, she made a passing fair boy, slim, with the square jaw of the Broomes, as her grandfather had told her, and the same dark brows. And Moll had cut her hair well. She had misled people in Oxfordshire and the rogues, too. But now she had gulled the practiced eyes of players into thinking she was Robin, not Rosalind. She laughed for an instant, then thought of Helen and Ned, caught that morning in the goldsmith's house. She thought of her flight through Blackfriars, of the forger, of Moll's friendship and Tom o' Bedlam's wrath, of the Earl of Essex, the play, Master Gulliford, and now Thomas Pope. What a day it had been! Yet she was not tired. She had never felt so alive in all her days.

Suddenly her mirror gazing was interrupted by Pope's shouting from below. "Robin, 'tis time to ride back to the playhouse."

Rosalind found the stage of the Curtain lit by candles set on the floor outlining its rim and by many torches in sconces at its rear. It was chill inside for all that it was late summer. Ice-white stars glittered through the opening at the Curtain's top. She was grateful for the warmth of the cloak Dame Gillet had given her, as she went about the chars Pope set her. In the tiring room she learned that an efficient company of players readied properties and costumes long before a play was performed. Tonight while the tiring men ironed and mended garments, Rosalind dusted off and repainted the face of the severed head she'd seen earlier that day. As she daubed paint on it, she watched Master Burbage striding about rehearsing gestures. He was crowned with a gilt circle, adorned with a false gray beard, and clad in the long scarlet gown of a king. What king, Rosalind had no idea. Then as she finished the head, she was called by Pope to attend Master Gulliford, who required his face to be painted again for another lady's part.

"What do I use?" she asked Gulliford as she looked bewildered at the many ointment pots on the table before him.

Seated on a high stool, he giggled. "The white paint. The white is the jawbones of a sow, burned, then mixed with oil of white poppy. Paint me first with the white. I shall darken my eyes with kohl and drop belladonna into them with this feather." He held up a white pigeon's feather, then glared across the tiring room at his uncle, who spoke with Master Will. Gulliford went on, "When I have donned my wig, I trust these players will think me a great lady enough for this old play. We only rehearse tonight. Master Burbage says he wishes to see how I will suit the lady's part. It is a new part for me."

As Rosalind began to stroke white onto the boy's face, she said, "I have met Dame Gillet. She is all that you say she is."

The boy player nodded sagely. "Do as I told you, Robin. Carry yourself cleverly. Master Pope may make a player of you yet. We have some need of boy players now. There are often too few of us. We come here as small lads and play women's roles until we are twenty years, if we can manage our voices that long. Some of us grow too tall much too quickly and grow beards." He smiled into the looking glass at his reflection. "Other boy players depart the company."

"Do all boys live with older players?"

"Aye, all do. I am older than you, Robin, near to sixteen. I shall not play court ladies much longer. I grow too old. I must have an eye to my future."

Rosalind had not guessed him to be so old. He was not tall. She went on smoothing the white stuff over his face, then asked, "Why do boys play women's parts?"

Gulliford did a strange thing. He pinched his stark white nose with his fingers and said, whining through it, " 'Boys must play women's parts. 'Tis a more scandalous thing for a woman to play a woman's part.' This is how many churchmen of London preach against us from their churches. They hate plays and players, but still we play. Someone must play women's parts. Authors keep writing parts into plays for women and girls. So boys and men must play them. Lads play pretty maidens and queens. Men play old women." He laughed. "You should see your good Master Pope play a fat old hag. You would not know him to be Master Pope at all."

Rosalind's work done with the white paint, the boy player waved her aside, motioned toward a scroll of paper, and then pulled a small pot of vermilion to him and began to paint his cheeks and lips with a brush. "Master Pope tells me you can read. I want to practice my lines for this play. Hear me recite them to you, Robin."

Rosalind unrolled the scroll. It was made up of sheets of paper pasted together. She saw lines of writing on it and in the left-hand margin instructions, "Enter," "Exit."

"Give me my cues," Gulliford commanded.

She felt helpless. "I do not know what cues are."

"They are the other player's closing lines to their speeches. Commence with the fourth line from the top. It should say, 'I'll win this Lady Margaret. For whom? Why, for my king. Tush! That's a wooden thing!'"

After Rosalind recited, Gulliford spoke his lines in an ice-sweet girlish treble. "'He talks of wood; it is some carpenter!' Now, Robin, you read the next line you see to me. After you have read it, I speak again."

For a half hour Rosalind coached Master Gulliford, who complained more than once that he was "slow of study." Then, snatching up a fan, the player, garbed as a dazzling, bewigged lady in a violet gown, swept out of the tiring room onto the stage.

All had gone out there now except for the tiring men, who folded costumes into chests. They paid no heed to Rosalind as she took up a candle and began to wander around the playhouse. First she read the pasteboard plot of *The Taming of the Shrew* hanging from a peg, listing the players' names. Then she found stairs leading down below the stage. There, as she listened to Burbage's resonant voice from above, she saw more steps. These steps led up to a trapdoor cut into the stage floor. Rosalind yearned to open it and poke her head through it to surprise the players but discarded the idea. She suspected Burbage would not approve if she interrupted his rehearsal. Because it was dark and gloomy under the stage, she soon left. She went back to the tiring room and began to climb another set of stairs she'd also spied out. They led above the stage to the hut. In it over the stage's ceiling, which was painted to represent a blue but clouded sky, she found a remarkable variety of things—a winch and a chairlike throne on ropes, a gray rain cloud of painted canvas, gunpowder in small casks, cannonballs, and a small cannon.

Also to her surprise she found Master Will seated at a small table, writing, flanked by two candles blowing slantwise in the August breeze.

Rosalind apologized, backing toward the steep flight of steps. "I did not mean to disturb you, sir."

He put his finger to his lips. "Do not tell anyone that I am here. I came up without their knowing it. They think I have gone home. Here I have some peace. In the tiring room I am besieged by players who say to me 'Alter this line for me' or 'Why have you given me but one song to sing in your new play?' " He laughed, then asked, "How do you fare with Master Pope?"

"I like him very well. I hope he may make a player of me. I would rather be a player than a servant."

The playwright nodded. "He has made players of other boys before. I am told you are a pastor's grandson, of good birth, read and write, and know Latin and Greek."

Rosalind felt her face grow hot. She could only nod. Master Pope had said much of her to the company in a very short time, it seemed, while she had repainted the earl's cut-off head.

He pushed a piece of blank paper over to her, then offered her his quill and ink. "Write these words for me as I speak them, Robin. Write in your very fairest hand."

Leaning over his table, Rosalind wrote as fast as she could in the hand her grandfather had taught her.

But when the blast of war blows in our ears,
Then imitate the action of the tiger;

Stiffen the sinews, summon up the blood. . . .

Master Will took the paper, looked at it, then nodded. "It is a fair secretary hand, the Italian hand. I write but the common English hand. Yours is by far the clearest I have seen of this company, and it is well spelled, too. Tell Master Pope for me that I shall require you to copy out the players' parts for the cue sheets for the play I now write."

Rosalind felt a pang of disappointment. First servant's work, now a clerk's.

"You do not wish to be a copyist for me?" Master Will seemed to have read her mind.

"If I am to be a servant to one player and a copyist to another, when am I to be a player?"

The playwright laughed. "Before you are a player, you will do many, many things. You will learn to starch ruffs, take playbills to the printer, nail them up on London Bridge, send this throne of the gods down out of our painted heavens by means of the winch, and push ghosts up through the trapdoor so their draperies will not get caught on the steps. Perhaps you will even set flame to the touch-hole of our cannon when the play calls for cannon fire, though I trust you will not send a ball through the roof or set the playhouse afire. Players must know all about the theater." The dark-eyed man rose, went to one end of the hut, and with his foot sent the cannonball rolling noisily across the floor. He put his finger to his lips again for silence.

"You up there in the hut! Cease that. We require no thunder in this play!" came Richard Burbage's angry roaring from the stage below.

Master Will waited until Rosalind had stopped laughing, then said, "Tell Dame Gillet to have your face washed well at the moon's wane with elder leaves distilled in May. You have country freckles, Robin."

Rosalind grinned; he but teased her. "'Tis near September now, and I'm not often out-of-doors. Freckles will go away."

"Yes, it is near autumn. Soon the Queen will return to London to spend the winter. She goes from London in the summer when the plague is most fierce."

"Do common folk ever see her, Master Will?"

"All London may see her if they choose to when she returns. She comes riding into the city with her court about her."

"Lord Essex, too? I saw him today."

The man's wise eyes were fixed on her face. "Aye, Essex, too. I do not know what business brought him here today. He is mostly with the Queen. You love him then?"

"Yes, he is the greatest man in England. My father was in Spain with him."

"Aye, the greatest man in England." His face grave, Master Will looked down at the papers of his unfinished play. "Many young men and all London lads love Essex well today. Tomorrow he may not fare so well."

Thomas Pope was not at all ill-pleased when he heard that Rosalind was to serve Master Will as well as himself. "Aye, you will learn much from him," he told her, "but do not forget ye serve me first. Each morning you will bring my beef, bread, and beer to me. You will do what errands Dame Gillet requires." The old player went on half scolding. "Robin, you will also rub your teeth each morning with the tooth blanch and a cloth to keep out the worms. I see you neglect them. All my player lads did so."

"Aye, Master Pope." Rosalind breathed deep with happiness. She was content with the old player, and she felt safe from Tom o' Bedlam, too. Sometimes in the days she stayed with the players she had thought with guilt of Cowley and her grandfather. No, there was truly nothing to keep her from going there and deserting Pope, but the matter of the book remained. Did her grandfather believe she had stolen it? More than likely he did. It would be best to return with another copy. Deep down in her heart Rosalind admitted the real reason for her tarrying so long in London. She was afraid to return, afraid to face Pastor Broome and the awful Dr. Hornsby, even with a copy of the book in hand. And what story would she tell them?

Days passed, very busy ones. When Pope learned how very swiftly Rosalind memorized and how quick her wits were, he began to teach her things. First he taught her to put her speaking voice to a steady high, piercing sweetness. Then he sent her, to her great joy, to a fencing master across the Thames on Ludgate Hill. Rosalind, who had always been interested, threw herself wholeheartedly into the study of swordsmanship, though at first she was afraid that the fencing master would guess she was a girl. He did not. He saw chiefly the shillings Pope gave him to teach her.

Pulling a boy's flat cap down over her head and striding boldly along, Rosalind soon learned that not one man of the City Watch paid her any heed.

Nary a word did Pope say to her of fashioning her into

a player. However, each day that passed she took more and more hope of it. When he started to teach her to gesture in a grand manner to show pity, anger, and grief, she felt she was on the path she sought. Dame Gillet also started to take a hand in her teaching. She taught her endless melancholy ballads of faithless young lovers, which made Rosalind want to yawn. Before long Rosalind could sing to a lute while Master Pope played the tenor viol and Dame Gillet the cithern. But it soon became clear to everyone, including Rosalind who had always known it, that she would never be a nightingale. "You will charm few serpents from their holes with your voice," Pope told her more than once.

Mistress Willingson, who had also said nothing to Rosalind about her aims, raised her hopes even higher one day when she began to show her how to play the part of a court lady. This was not easy for country-bred Rosalind, who, though she had worn petticoats, had never worn a wide farthingale skirt before and who did not know how to use a fan. She didn't know how to laugh sweetly and flirt. Dame Gillet scolded her over and over. "Robin, you are clumsy, more clumsy than the other lads Master Pope has asked me to instruct. Pay heed! You must curtsey *so*, sinking down and holding your skirt." When Dame Gillet said she was satisfied, Rosalind was aware that she now knew what Lady Margaret Forster would have taught her in Oxfordshire. She knew, too, that learning from Dame Gillet was far more pleasant. Dame Gillet laughed now and then.

Pope's housekeeper did not try to teach her the dances of London fashion. That was done by a mincing little French dancing master in Blackfriars to whom she took another shilling in payment each Tuesday morning. He taught her the coranto and the galliard, the man's paces as well as the woman's for Pope said she must know them both. Certainly this requirement meant that Pope had it in mind to make a player of her!

At all of these things Rosalind worked hard, so hard that she was often too wearied with them and her duties for Pope and for Master Will to think overmuch of Cowley or to write a letter to her grandfather. What if he should come after her? It was the sort of thing he would do. No, at the moment she wanted no one in Cowley to know where she was or what she was doing.

Martin Sclater met with his master at a tavern in Fleet Street late in October. Adam Fenchurch came to the upper room where his servant waited and flung his wet cloak over the back of a chair before he went to warm his hands at the hearth.

"I've come from the Queen's palace," he told Sclater. "I have claimed the barony of Broome. What news do you have for me of the girl Rosalind?"

Sclater shook his head. "None at all, master. I have been to every part of the city and to Southwark as well as to the fields outside the city. It is as if she has been swallowed up —that is, if she came to London at all."

Fenchurch frowned, looking into the flames, then said, "Perhaps she came here and died. There was some plague about in the city in July."

"No, master. I have checked parish registers. No girl named Broome has died. Master, could she be still in Oxfordshire?"

Fenchurch shook his head. "No, Martin. I have had men searching there also. One man learned a thing that could be of import to you. This Rosalind Broome sometimes garbed herself as a boy, and as a lad she would not have called herself Rosalind. And she spoke often to people of visiting London. Perhaps she came here as a lad and is playing still as one?"

Sclater thought of the boy he'd seen riding double with the large man on Fish Street. Could that have been the girl he sought? "Do you know what name she took?"

"God's blood, Martin, who would know that? The man who learned in Cowley that she fancies wearing boy's garments said she was a bold and willful wench. The sort of girl who would run away and seek her fortune in London as a lad might. I think she came here and is here still, but she is playing the part of a boy."

"That changes matters."

"It does indeed." Fenchurch pondered a moment. "Martin, leave off your searching here now. Go you to Cowley to learn what more you can of her. And ask, too, for her in Oxford. Her grandfather, I am told, was a friend of the Master of Corpus Christi, Dr. Hornsby. Talk to Hornsby of her. He may know her. He may know her wont."

"Aye, Master Fenchurch, I will go in the morning."

Church bells, hundreds of them, pealing together rang in mid-November the day the Queen reentered London. With thousands of other people Rosalind came to stand beneath Charing Cross to see her pass. Queen Elizabeth entered the city from the west, this time riding in an open litter, not on horseback. Four hundred worthy Londoners in velvet cloaks, with golden chains about their necks, rode before her as an escort. Behind her came the nobles of her court, glittering gorgeously with jewels, costly clothing, and hat plumes of every color under the sun. With thousands of others Rosalind cheered, throwing up her cap, but it was not only for the Queen she cheered. On the Queen's right hand in the place of honor rode the Earl of Essex, mounted on his beautiful black horse. She caught only a tiny glimpse of the old Queen, who was huddled against the sharp day in a mantle of black furs. She saw only red hair and a long pointed nose. But she could see Essex well, shining like the summer sun in cloth of gold, his head bare to the wintry winds.

Other folk loved him well, too. Rosalind heard a man standing behind her say, "Would that Lord Essex shared the throne with the Queen. She is more than sixty years old. Still the witch will not name who is to rule us when she dies. I do not like it. I do not like her Sir Robert Cecil, the hunchback, who spins his spider webs in Whitehall Palace, though the Queen likes him well enough. More than that I mislike the news out of Ireland. We win no victories there with our armies against the Irish rebels."

The man next to him, a portly Londoner, said, "Perhaps the Queen will send Lord Essex there with another army. He will crush the wild Irish."

Rosalind paid scant heed to them, though the word *witch* had caught her ear and made her think of Moll and the rogues. She followed the citizens away, then made her way to the private indoor playhouse in Blackfriars, which the Lord Chamberlain's Company used in cold weather. She was to watch the players rehearsing this afternoon.

Master Pope had taken a new step. Now he commanded her at every opportunity to learn from the players. First she wanted to see Master Will. His new play was finished. It was to be performed for the very first time at the new playhouse Burbage planned to erect out of the timbers of the old Theatre in Holywell Fields.

Today, her cap in her hand, Rosalind came to the tiring room to find the playwright. Her heart beat very fast. She had a great favor to ask of him. It had been growing in the back of her mind while she copied out the cue sheets for the new play. She waited until he gave her his full attention, then she dared speak to him. "Master Will, I know I am not a player yet. But will there be a part for me in the new play? Master Pope and Dame Gillet have taught me very much."

He nodded, but this time did not smile at her. "They have, I know, and you have made good progress, I hear. But Tom Pope tells me you are not yet ready to go before the London folk, who have been known to pelt players who displeased them with dead cats." He touched her arm gently, comforting her, and said, "Yet I believe I may find somewhat for you to do. Perhaps you shall beat the drum and perhaps you can enter with the Princess of France as one of the ladies of her court. Can you manage skirts and petticoats well as yet?"

"Dame Gillet has done her best to teach me."

"Then you shall be seen by London in the springtime at the new playhouse, though no one will hear you—except as the voice of a drum."

On the last day of November Dame Gillet, who felt an

ague coming on her, sent Rosalind in her place to the just-finished Royal Exchange to buy velvet ribbands and copper lace to trim an old gown. Rosalind climbed to the Exchange's famous upper pawn, where musicians played constant sprightly airs and where a person could buy anything from beard brushes and picktooths to silver pouncet-boxes and pomanders. She purchased the lace and ribbands and was about to go home to Southwark when she heard a babble of voices and caught the words, " 'Tis Lord Essex himself!"

Rosalind darted out of the draper's shop. Aye, it was true. The earl, wrapped in a long mantle of black, came striding along the upper pawn, nodding and smiling at the people who greeted him. Other men walked behind him, also smiling and nodding.

Rosalind seized her second chance. She stepped out into the corridor and sweeping off her cap went down onto one knee. This time she found her tongue. Master Pope and Dame Gillet had taught her what to say. "My lord, let me speak with you."

Essex had a smile for her. "What would you say to me, boy?"

"My father sailed with you to Spain. He died there. Did you know him? He was of Oxfordshire, of Cowley, and named Henry Broome. I am Robin Broome."

The earl touched her shoulder. "I did not know him. There were many, many brave Englishmen with me when we raided the Spanish port of Cadiz. I am sorry that your father did not return." He reached down and pulled Rosalind up by the hand. "What do you now so far from Oxfordshire?"

"I learn to be a player, my lord."

"Ah, now I see why you speak so fairly. With what company?"

"The Lord Chamberlain's."

Essex nodded. "I find that very well. You will bring merriment to this world. It has great need of it." Essex turned to the man next to him. "I envy this little player lad. He need never fear a knife in the dark from envious men as I do. What enemy could this child have?"

VI

ROBIN A DALE

December, 1598, was cold, the most fearful winter in many years, complained Thomas Pope, who declared his bones were "chilled to the very marrow." In the middle of the month the Thames froze solid, so Rosalind and her master crossed the city to Blackfriars on horseback over the ice. Later in December it snowed. Christmas day was bitter chill but a happy one for Rosalind, for that day she left the company of the stableboy, porter, and the kitchen maids to sit at Pope's table. This, she hoped, was another step forward to becoming a player and the accumulation of the money which would permit her to buy a copy of the stolen book. Servants earned but little, and the book, which she had already priced, was very costly.

With Dame Gillet and Pope, Rosalind sat in Saint Saviour's Church under the holly and the ivy on Christmas day watching her own frosty breath. She wondered how her grandfather fared in Cowley. Perhaps if she could find someone trustworthy traveling to Oxfordshire, she would send a letter to him, telling that she fared well but giving no inkling of where she was or what she was doing. She stayed in Southwark the day after Christmas while the Lord Chamberlain's Company went to Whitehall Palace to play before the Queen, no novelty to them. With Dame Gillet, who knitted, she waited before the warm fire until Pope returned, shaking the new snow from his hooded mantle.

"How did you find the Queen tonight?" asked Dame Gillet.

"Well enough. She favored our play, which she had not seen before, and smiled whenever I spoke my lines. We play before her again on January first, as you. . . ."

Because she knew her master well and did not fear his rage, which was more wind than passion, Rosalind interrupted with a question. "Did you also see Lord Essex tonight, master?"

Pope would not be hurried. He sat down in his chair and took up the hot mulled wine ready for him and drank it half down before he answered. "I saw the Queen, who is his cousin, dance with him. He is much in her favor now. 'Tis said she will send him soon to Ireland with an army to fight the rebels." Pope finished the wine and said to Rosalind, "In two days' time, Robin, we shall remove the old Theatre from Holywell Fields here to Southwark. Burbage will leave that scoundrel who owns the land with naught but his barren ground. It will pay him out nicely because he would not renew the lease."

Rosalind shook her head. "Who will take the Theatre down?" How incredible she found this plan.

"A clever carpenter of London. We players shall aid him."

"Who is to pay for this removal?" asked Dame Gillet.

"Burbage and five of us. Will Shakespeare, Will Kemp, two others, and myself. Each shall own shares in the new playhouse. It and the plays Master Will plans to write will make us richer than we now are, dame."

Before dawn of the twenty-eighth Rosalind arrived with Pope at the snowy fields north of London. They found others had arrived before them, working by torchlight, making a frightful clamor. The carpenter, his journeymen, and apprentices were already busily dismantling the Theatre. With axes and with swords the players, who came singly and in pairs, set about helping them. Because she had cut much wood in Cowley for her ailing grandfather, Rosalind plied the axe, which the carpenter had given her, with some skill. She was pleased when Pope, who hacked away puffing with a sword, called out to her, "Well done, Robin!" Once even Burbage gave her a smile as he passed by.

By dusk of that same day the Theatre was down, and the last of the carts loaded with timbers were on their way to the Thames to be taken across to Southwark's marshes. Hot and weary but very well satisfied by their day's hard work, the players went to Bread Street to the noisy, food-scented Mermaid tavern for wine. Thanks to her yeoman work with an axe, Richard Burbage ordered Rosalind brought a cup of hot wine and a great beef pie, near a foot wide.

She heard him ask Henry Condell over the music of the inn's pipers and fiddlers, "Where was your young Gulliford today?"

"Lying warm abed, his head under the coverlets," grumbled Condell. "Bones o' God, I do not know what is amiss with him. He says I do not give him the full wages due him, though I know I do. I keep out only money to buy him clothing. He does not fancy hard labor. My little Davey is ailing or he would have come willingly."

The rough-tongued little clown of the company, Will Kemp, spoke up next. He pointed to Rosalind. "Tom Pope has the better apprentice. Robin worked right well today."

"I do believe I have at that," said the player.

Rosalind's heart grew so full at the praise that she almost choked on the last bite of her pie. Before nearly all the company, Pope had claimed her as a "player's apprentice."

"Give us an air, Robin?" Kemp asked Rosalind, whose cheeks still flamed with pleasure at her master's long-hoped-for words.

"Aye, sing for us," commanded Burbage. "Perhaps Tom Pope has better taught you to sing than to dance."

Rosalind glanced at Pope. "Shall I, Master Pope?"

"Aye, go to it, lad. If you squeak after such a day's chill work, no man will hold it against you. Say your throat pains you. And in such tumult as this tavern, who will hear you?"

Rosalind did not see her master wink at Kemp, as the host of the Mermaid brought a lute to her. The players all knew what would happen. All heads turned at once toward the players' table. The tavern fell silent, hoping for entertainment. Horrified, Rosalind would have sat down again but dared not. Catching her master's encouraging nod, she began to play the lute. After a moment's faltering, she launched into an old ballad of Robin Hood and Sherwood Forest. From great Burbage to the most humble potboy all listened. When she finished no man hissed or mewed. Many applauded her but not one man of the Lord Chamberlain's Company.

"The lad progresses," said Burbage to Pope, "but as yet I doubt if he is ready for a part in a play. And no man could say he has the voice of an angel, though it is still high enough."

"I have had him but four months' time, Richard," protested the old player.

"In that small time I would say Robin bears well." Master Will who had been silent up till now added, "He will play parts sooner than you might think." The playwright was always kind to the youngest players. Rosalind blessed him in her heart for it.

Burbage looked appraisingly at her. "You are called Robin?"

"Robin Broome, sir, as you would like it."

"I like it not. That name limps upon my tongue."

"I am sorry, Master Burbage."

"It must be altered. If you are to be a player, as Will says you are, you require a name folk like to speak. What do you fancy?" The great player sounded amused.

Rosalind looked helplessly at her master, who puffed upon his pipe and shrugged. Master Will answered for her. "His song just put me in mind of something. True, he can scarce sing like Robin Hood's minstrel, Alan a Dale, but I have always favored that name." He leaned forward, his dark eyes on Rosalind. "Would you like to be called Robin a Dale after Robin Hood's friend? Londoners would well remember that name where they would not recall Robin Broome. Broome will make folk think of sweeping."

Rosalind didn't hesitate for an instant. Like every other child in England, she loved the outlaws of Sherwood Forest. "Aye, Master Will, I would indeed."

Pope lifted his cup of wine. "And if your grandfather or any other man comes to London seeking you as Robin Broome, he'll not find Robin a Dale."

"Who would come seeking me?" asked Rosalind, but a pang knifed through her as she thought of Cowley and the journey there she kept postponing. If her grandfather could see her supping with "common players" at this moment he would not only be disgraced but would surely think that the Devil the London rogues spoke of familiarly, as if he were a man, had her fast in his foul clutches.

Returned from Oxfordshire, Martin Sclater had spent that bitterly cold day snug in his usual chamber at the inn in Fleet Street. As Rosalind had finished the last notes of her song, Sclater took up his quill and dipped it into ink. He frowned at the sheet of paper before him. By rights he should send a letter to his master in Saint Albans, telling him that more weeks of hard searching had not yet found either girl or boy who might be Rosalind Broome. And Dr. Hornsby at Corpus Christi College in Oxford had told him nothing except that Pastor Broome's granddaughter was well educated and that she had gone to a play and then disappeared with his book. And often she dressed as a boy!

So little news would anger Fenchurch greatly. He did not fancy hearing "no" at any time from any man, less so from his servants. Better by far to let Master Fenchurch believe by his silence that his servant hunted still for the child, as truly he did.

Martin shook the hair out of his eyes, No, he decided he would not write a letter at all. Instead, to remind himself, he would list places where he could most likely spy out the girl—or the girl masking as a lad. He'd been often to the menagerie at the Tower of London and to the gardens of Whitehall, both places frequented by the public. Three times each week he had gone to Duke Humphrey's Walk in Saint Paul's to scan faces of the children who came there. He'd gone to the guildhalls of the merchants to run his finger down the lists of new apprentices for a "Broome." He'd looked hard at dirty-faced kitchen wenches, inn pot-boys, and stable lads wherever he went. But no man or woman had seen the accursed brat. It was as if she had been drowned deep in the Thames.

He dipped his quill again, and he wrote for his own use: "Visit Duke Humphrey's Walk *each* day." Then beneath this he scratched, "Go to the Royal Exchange *each* day."

Aye, if he had not marked out Rosalind Broome and dealt with her before winter passed, he would haunt other places popular with Londoners in the spring. The play-houses and Bear Garden of Southwark would reopen then after Lent. No matter how well hid the girl might be in London now, she probably would be lured across the Thames in the springtime by the dogs, bears, and players. Young bold wenches and all lads loved the entertainments rowdy Southwark offered.

And very bold this Rosalind must be to steal a valuable book from old Hornsby. A man who had dared to lecture Queen Elizabeth to her face would not hesitate to see a thief hang. This was a piece of news that would interest Fenchurch. Yes, he would write him that.

Martin took a second sheet of paper and wrote: "The girl I seek to give your loving greetings to, Master Fenchurch, stole a book of great worth from the Master of Corpus Christi College. It is no small wonder that she hides herself so well from your servant. But rest easy. I shall find her."

Early in February, some days after her thirteenth birthday, Rosalind went walking with her master and Dame Gillet. "The day is fine and 'tis not far to Maiden Lane. Shall we see how the building of the new playhouse fares?" suggested Pope.

Dame Gillet laughed. "As if you do not go there every other day, Thomas, and drag poor Robin with you when he should be helping me. You can scarce wait for the gilders to be done with the building so that penny stinkards can come across the Thames with their pennies to hand."

Their affectionate bickering, which amused Rosalind, continued as they walked along the Bankside. She welcomed their raillery, for it raised her spirits. On Sunday afternoons such as this one she thought much of Cowley. Often she was able to push memories of her grandfather out of her mind, but Sundays were difficult. On Sundays she felt most guilty. She should go home, but truly she didn't want to. She loved the world of plays and players and found pleasure in the company of Pope and his housekeeper. No, she could never know such joy in tiny Cowley, where her grandfather scolded her constantly and overgodly Lady Margaret Forster expected to have her come live with her.

Rosalind tried to listen to Pope and Dame Gillet but

could not keep her mind on their words for thinking of her grandfather. She was relieved when they came to the high eight-sided wooden building reared on piles out of the Southwark marsh. The new playhouse was much like those of Holywell Fields. Its roof was also of thatch but inside, as she had already seen, it was far finer than the Curtain or the Theatre had been. Much gold paint was being used to brighten it. The stage pillars were to be painted to resemble costly Italian marble. Already a clever man with an eye to making a profit from thirsty playgoers was building an alehouse next door. Because the new playhouse was to be so very splendid, it was taking much time to be readied.

Inasmuch as it was Sunday, no painters or gilders were at work, but a voice hailed them all the same. Out from the building strolled Kemp, the renowned clown of the company. With him came a stranger. He was tall with curling black hair, a wide nose, and pockmarked face. For all that he walked with a swagger, his clothing was poor brown leather and wool. To Rosalind's eye, he had the look of a canting man.

She felt Dame Gillet stiffen beside her. Under her breath the woman told Pope, "'Tis Ben Jonson."

"Tut, woman," said Pope. To Jonson he called out after he bowed, "How do you fare, Master Jonson?"

"Ah, Master Pope. I am again out of prison. I have escaped the hangman's rope to the joy of some and the sorrow of others, and I have suffered only this," said Jonson in a loud voice, holding out his right thumb. On it Rosalind saw a healing burn. "I am writing a play for your company. When will this fine playhouse of Master Burbage's be finished?" At this point the man swept off his hat and bowed to Mistress Willingson. Turning back to Pope, he asked, "Will you take a cup of ale with me at the Falcon?"

After a grudging curtsey and a shake of her head, Dame Gillet went into the playhouse. Pope said as he followed her, "Come April the playhouse will be ready. I am very pleased to hear you write a play for us, Master Ben. I will meet you at the Falcon in an hour's time."

"Master, who was that man? Is he a rogue?" asked Rosalind inside. Among the canting folk she'd sometimes seen the Tyburn Mark, the branded thumb, which meant its bearer was a murderer who had claimed "the benefit of clergy" because he could read and write. Such men were not hanged as others were.

Dame Gillet answered her and sniffed as she did. "Ben Jonson. Aye, he is a rogue. It is because of men like him that players have evil names among many folk. Once he was in prison for a scandalous play he wrote offending the Queen and now again for killing a player in a duel. Master Jonson has enough conceit for two men. Leave him be, Robin."

Pope laughed at her. "Tut, Jonson's comedies have wit, dame. London likes them. Perhaps Robin will have his first part in one of them."

Rosalind kept her silence. She had not told her master that she had a promise from Master Will that she could have a part in his new play for all that she had no lines to speak. Pope showed Dame Gillet a fine, bright-painted signboard propped up along the bottom of the rear gallery, waiting to be put up. It showed a man who carried the world upon his shoulders. "This is to be our signboard, dame. The Globe is what we will name the playhouse. The man, you see, carries the globe on his shoulders."

Dame Gillet gazed thoughtfully at the very sharp colors of the signboard, then said, "'Tis bright enough to be seen across the Thames in Blackfriars. What are the words beneath the man and the globe? I do not know what they mean."

Rosalind explained. "They are in Latin, dame. They are *Totus mundus agit histrionen.* Their meaning is 'All the world's a stage.' "

"It is not every player who has an apprentice who has Latin," Pope boasted. "Garb Robin here in cloth of silver and velvet, and I think he could play the part ere long of a noble young lord."

Rosalind's laugh was uncomfortable. As the watchman of the Globe saw them out, she thought of her kinsman who was a lord. This she kept secret still from Pope. No players she had met among the Lord Chamberlain's Company were rogues, but none were nobles either, though Shakespeare and Pope claimed gentle birth. Rosalind knew in her heart that they would not have accepted her if they were aware of her kinship with a peer. In her first days in London she had gone with the nip and jostler to stand outside the House of Lords in the hopes that she might spy out her grandfather's older brother, Lord Broome. But she had not found him. An old man, standing next to her, had named, one by one, every lord who went inside the House of Lords but not once had he muttered, "Broome."

She had finally asked him if he knew aught of Baron Broome. He had told her, "Aye, my girl, but I have not seen him for many years. He is very old—too old to ride to London."

Late in March while the Globe's interior was still being

readied and Rosalind still working hard to become a player, the Earl of Essex started for Ireland in charge of an army. Every lad in London thrilled to the news. The tavern talk was of nothing but Essex, who would put down the Irish rebels for all time. The twenty-seventh was the day set for him to march out of London with an army of a hundred and sixty bands of foot soldiery and twenty-six of cavalry. That day Rosalind could not work at her player's gesturing. She could not put her wits to anything but the departure of the man her father had served under. In a fever she asked Pope to let her cross to London to see him go. He sighed and told her, "Aye, go."

Long before she reached Cornhill in London Rosalind heard the cheering and shouting and the thunder of drums. Finally she struggled through the massed citizens to see the soldiers raised for Ireland passing. Some trailed twenty-foot pikes while others carried billhooks. Strutting brown-faced archers wore padded jackets and carried full quivers and bows. Musketeers paraded past with arquebuses and small petronels. The music of fife and drum came, alas, from somewhere at the head of the procession. That is where Lord Essex would be.

She had missed him! But she knew the army marched that day to Islington, outside the city. In a flash she ducked back through the throng, running west. Aye, she might see the earl at Cheapside if she made haste. Out of breath, she again pushed her way through the crowd. To her joy she saw him, riding in silver-gilt half armor at the head of his army. With half of London she shouted, "God save your Lordship! God preserve your honor!" Then when the soldiers had passed, she straggled down Cheapside after them. Four miles trailing the army she walked in company with several hundred London lads. She would have gone farther on the long road to Ireland except at Islington the fair day turned suddenly foul. In a few minutes the sky blackened and lightning started to fork across it, followed by thunder. An ice-cold hail beat down after the first cannon-clap of thunder.

Scowling, getting more wet with each step, Rosalind went back with the earl's other admirers to London. Near London Bridge her foot slipped on a water-streaming cobblestone. As she lurched forward, she felt a sudden tug at her purse. Her hand shot out swiftly and caught a small, cold wet one fast in her own.

"Rosalind," cried the nip, looking up into her face.

"Aye, pick another purse than mine, Dickon," she snapped.

"I swear it. I did not know 'twas ye, or I'd not done it. Ye've got so very fine." Dickon gazed admiringly at her good brown cloak. "I followed ye from Islington fer yer purse. I could not mark out yer face wi' yer hat pulled so low."

Rosalind was wet and weary and in no mood to talk with Dickon. Her throat ached from cheering. She reached into her purse and gave the nip and jostler each a penny. She was about to turn away and cross to Southwark when she noticed that the jostler was standing on tiptoe to whisper into Dickon's ear.

The nip listened, then nodded. "I near forget to tell ye. There was a man give me a groat in Saint Paul's last week for news of a lad or a wench named Broome."

Rosalind's heart almost stopped. "Was he very old? Was he a pastor in a long black gown?"

"Na. He asked fer a 'Broome o' Cowley in Oxfordshire.'

He said he was 'neighbor' to ye there. He was swart wi' a black fork beard an' scars an' burns on th' backs o' his hands. I looks well at men's hands, bein' as a nip is my trade."

Rosalind shook her head. "I know no one in Cowley who is like that. What did you tell him, Dickon?"

The boy chuckled. "That I knew ye not. 'Twas but a groat he give me. If he'd made free wi' a shillin' I mighta told him somewhat of ye, but I think not. He coulda been sent by the City Watch to find ye." Dickon reached out to touch the cloth of her warm cloak. He fingered it as if he wanted it. Rosalind thought of giving it to him, but decided not to though he seemed blue with cold. It might anger her master and Dame Gillet if she did. She had but one cloak. The jostler was as cold as Dickon.

"Rosalind, what do ye now?" asked Dickon, while the icy rain trickled down his filthy face, washing clean rivulets in it.

"I'm with the Lord Chamberlain's Company of players."

The nip's jaw dropped, and his mouth fell open into an astonished *O*. "Ye are, Rosalind? Ye be with Master Burbage at the playhouse? Ye play parts?"

"I hope to play many parts. The players take me for a lad."

The jostler as well as Dickon was gaping at her now. "Ye gulled Master Burbage and the players?" Dickon hugged himself, doubled over with laughter. He pointed at her. "Ye gulled Tom o' Bedlam. Ye gulled the Watch of London, and now ye gull players." He tilted Rosalind's cap back to peer into her face. "Ye do look to be more of a lad than a wench at that. Ye did not make a pretty maid, as I remembers ya."

Not caring much for his overhonest comment, Rosalind pulled her cloak away from Dickon's grasp. "Tell Moll for me what I do now. She asked me not to come to her at Whitefriars."

The nip nodded. "I'll tell her."

"What of the Upright Man? Does he still lead the canting men?"

"He does. I'll tell him of ye too if ye wish it."

The girl shrugged. "I do not think he would take much interest in me, Dickon."

"Na," agreed the boy. "When I see him at the Holy Lamb or Gun, he talks mostly o' the Devil with Moll or Tom o' Bedlam."

Rosalind shivered. She asked, "Is Tom often in London Town, Dickon?"

"Tom comes and Tom goes out again," volunteered the jostler.

All at once Rosalind asked them, "What does Tom do in the country?"

Dickon answered her, "I know not. Moll warned us to be wary of him and of the Devil's business. Tom likes Moll little and has no kind words for nips and anglers. Kyncheon coves let Tom o' Bedlam be."

"What of Ned and Helen?" asked Rosalind.

The nip explained while the jostler looked up into the streaming sky. "Caught wi' Kate, who played the part of kitchen maid to the goldsmith. You had the right of it, Rosalind. 'Twas a snare of the City Watch. They had no luck atall. They was all hanged—hanged the same day at Tyburn Gallows. I saw it done." He touched her cloak again. "Some players I hear be rich folk. Master Burbage is a rich man. Ye do have luck, Rosalind."

The girl looked into the nip's shrewd eyes. She knew what Dickon wanted. She sighed deeply, then told him, "Cut my purse, Dickon." It had a shilling and three more pennies in it.

The nip cut it with his dagger but did not take it. She handed it to him wordlessly. She was well fed and warm. A good meal and a blazing hearth awaited her over the Thames in Pope's Southwark house. The two little rogues were ragged as ever and unless things had changed greatly in Moll's house, probably hungry, too.

She told Dickon as she started away, "Angle for warm cloaks for you and the jostler."

Her head bent against the downpour, Rosalind left the rogues on her way to London Bridge. Master Pope and Dame Gillet would not beat her if she told them someone had cut off her purse in the great throng that cheered Lord Essex.

As she walked under the black shadows of the bridge she asked herself why would anyone seek her in London? Who was it? Was it some stranger her grandfather had sent after her? Or was the man with scars on his hands sent from Dr. Hornsby, who wanted his book? This "neighbor from Cowley" said he looked for a girl—or a lad. Both old men knew she went about as a lad.

The clang of the great bell of Saint Saviour's greeted her as she entered Southwark. As she passed the churchyard, she saw black-clad mourners and a coffin green-strewn with bay, the holy cross carried before it. While thunder clamored overhead, she dropped to her knees in the muddy lane, as was the custom, to pray for the soul of the dead stranger. She wondered why a man who came from Cowley might be seeking her. Had her grandfather sent someone to hunt for her in London?

By the fifteenth of April Burbage's gilders pronounced the Globe finished. Rosalind bubbled with excitement. She'd reminded Master Will of his promise that she was to beat the drum and act the part of a lady in *Henry V*. But not one word would she have to speak. Aye, he was to tell Pope at once of this agreement with her, and Robin a Dale, the player, was to sign a paper that he would do "all things" other players did. Robin a Dale would attend all rehearsals, pay small fines if he was late or did not appear and an enormous one if he should arrive for a performance too drunk to play his part. She signed the paper before some of the players and with them laughed at her master's warning, "If you come drunken, you will forfeit very much, Robin. Drink ale before you bear a part—never wine."

Days before the play Rosalind went to nail playbills on London Bridge. How wonderful it was to read the lists of players on it!

King Henry was Richard Burbage; the comical blustering Welshman, Fluellen, Thomas Pope; the Chorus, William Shakespeare; and the Princess of France, Master John Gulliford. But most wonderful of all, at the very bottom of the bills listed under Attendants to the Princess of France she saw the name Robin a Dale.

Rosalind could not sleep the night before the play for worry. She'd learned to beat a drum well enough, but would she stumble as she entered or made her exit? Could she get through the narrow doors of the stage easily in a farthingale hoop skirt, or would she get stuck? Would the tight corset she'd be laced into to give her a small waist make her cough? Would all London, armed with dead cats and old apples, laugh at her clumsiness?

At one o'clock folk came in a positive torrent across London Bridge and in the watermen's boats to pay out their pennies and shillings to the Globe's gatherers. They crowded the galleries and packed the pit, crying "ooh" and "ah" at the magnificence of Master Burbage's new theater. Trembling, Rosalind watched them through a peephole from the tiring room. She heard them cheer brave Burbage in his red robe as King Henry and bellow with laughter at Pope with the green leek of Wales stuck defiantly in his hat. But when the Princess of France swept across the stage with her ladies, all London went "ah" in unison at their great beauty. Rosalind had already beat the drum at her proper cue and not shamed her master. In this scene, tailing Gulliford, she walked as a court damsel and even curtseyed in her tawny silken skirts. No one laughed. She did not stumble nor did she cough. And too soon she had gone offstage back to the tiring room.

As she removed her high-piled headdress and wig she glanced at Master Will, who smiled at her. *Henry V* had been much admired by the Londoners. Now he had a new play in the writing. Perhaps there would be a speaking part, a very small one, in it for Robin a Dale. Rosalind knew she could not ask Pope to beg for her nor could she ask Master Gulliford, who day by day grew more sharp-tongued and bitter toward his uncle and the other players. No, she must bide her time and ask Shakespeare herself.

To remove her costume, Rosalind went into the grove of bay trees. Her modesty was a jest to the players. The tiring men had thought her mad at first, when she refused their services and got into her lady's gown alone and painted her face. Pope explained to them, "Young Robin is a pastor's grandson. Let him shift his clothing for himself. Otherwise, he will flush from his toenails to his eyebrows. Such a shy lad!"

May Day gave Rosalind the chance to talk privately with Shakespeare, when she went with some of the company to bring a Maypole into Southwark. While the other players searched for a tall straight tree, picked wild flowers, and cut green boughs, Rosalind sought out Master Will. She found him leaning on one elbow in the sunshine beside a brook, fishing. He looked up and sighed. "Robin, what do you seek? Why are you not gathering cuckoo flowers or violets?"

His words made her think fleetingly of Tom o' Bedlam and the innkeeper of Uxbridge, who had also spoken of flowers. The other comments had had some meaning that she could not fathom. Who was the Devil, for instance? But Master Will's question had been innocent. He went on, "Do not tell me why you have come to me today. I know. You seek a part in my new play?"

Embarrassed by the shrewd guess, Rosalind sat down beside him. She hung her head. "Yes, sir." Because she'd started copying cue scrolls for the new play, she knew that there were several women's parts in it. She knew Gulliford would play the chief one and more than likely Condell's other boy, younger than she, would bear a part also. He had been trained for two years now and still had never spoken a line.

"I think you might make a country wench or shepherdess," remarked Master Will. Rosalind noted how carefully he regarded her. "You have copied out the lines and cues for Phebe, have you not?"

Phebe? Phebe spoke words to an audience again and again. Phebe's part was no tiny one, though the girl named Rosalind, by coincidence someone of the same exact name as hers, was the true heroine of the play. She had no words of gratitude for the playwright. She could only look at him while her heart sang the music her voice could not manage. She felt her face reddening and looked from him to the brook, then said happily, "Master Will, I think there is a fine trout coming at your line."

Summer came. Though Thomas Pope had doubts that Rosalind was ready to play an important role, he gave in to Master Will's request and coached her long in the part of Phebe. The girl swiftly learned her own speeches, then helped Gulliford with the lines for Rosalind, the play's lively heroine. He showed little enthusiasm for the part and yawned often when he should have been studying. Many, many times over she repeated Rosalind's lines to him, so many times that her own rapid memory finally absorbed them. When one of the clowns deserted the company in midsummer, Master Gulliford crowed his pleasure at the other players' trouble in finding a replacement. Gulliford was clearly angry when an actor was found to play the fool Touchstone in the new play Master Will called *As You Like It*. It seemed to Rosalind that the boy player hated everyone in the Lord Chamberlain's Company. He even snarled at her.

The dawn of the tenth of July found Rosalind at the

Globe, waiting anxiously. Would it rain? She had prayed first that it would, then that it would not. But, no, the morning sky was blue and clear.

Dame Gillet, scolding, brought her food mid-morning, but she could not eat. She could only gnaw at her knuckles and go on muttering her lines or wander nervously about the playhouse. Costumed in the blue bodice and gray kirtle and petticoat of a shepherdess, wearing a black wig and with her face painted a sun brown, Rosalind was ready to go on stage by noon. Because she could not sit still in the tiring room, Burbage sharply ordered her out onto the stage to fidget where she would disturb no one else.

There seated in a gallery, reading a book, she found Ben Jonson. Since she had first met him with her master and Dame Gillet, she had come to know him better. He was far different from Master Will but all the same not unlikable. And rogues no longer frightened her very much. She wondered if he knew Tom o' Bedlam, Moll, or the Upright Man but never dared ask him. His wits were very sharp. He would wonder how she knew them. Jonson was a scholar for all of his rough appearance. He thought highly of lads like Robin a Dale, who had so much Latin poetry stuffed into their heads. "Master Robin, I see you play a part to-day?" he asked, hailing Rosalind.

"Aye, Master Jonson, I do."

"And you played a court lady in _Henry V,_ did you not?" When Rosalind had nodded, Jonson went on, "Perhaps there will be a part in the play I am writing for Robin a Dale if he speaks well today."

This suggestion caught Rosalind's attention at once. "Will there be many parts for ladies in it?"

"Two. Two most excellent parts. Tell me, have you played yet at some noble house or at court?"

Rosalind came down the steps, then across the pit to stand below the man, her bothersome shepherdess's crook hanging comically around her neck. "No, Master Jonson. Master Pope goes, but he has not taken me as yet."

"In time, I am sure you will go with him. The Queen favors players." Jonson leaned over the railing of the gallery and asked, "What think you of today's play by Master Will?"

Rosalind replied with care. She knew as all players knew that Jonson was somewhat jealous of Shakespeare. "I like it well enough." She was much relieved when Pope stuck his head out of one of the stage doors and bellowed for her to "come help Master Gulliford with his lines again."

That afternoon Rosalind moved about in a dream. When she heard her cue to enter, she went on stage even though her legs felt wooden and her heart pounded fast enough to burst. She played the proud shepherdess Phebe, mocking her would-be lover in a cruel manner. As Phebe she simpered at Gulliford's Rosalind, who was masquerading at times in the play as a lad. And when she came to the finest lines Master Shakespeare had written for Phebe, she took a deep breath as Tom Pope had taught her and said very sweetly and loudly, " 'Whoever lov'd that lov'd not at first sight?' " She was rewarded with a sigh of delight from the two thousand or more Londoners watching her and listening to her. Twice more Phebe came onstage, once to speak words of love to a mocking Rosalind and then at the end of the play to wed her shepherd lover.

Of a sudden the wondrous thing was finished and with

the others Rosalind had to leave the stage. Speaking a part had been a beauteous thing, too soon ended.

While Gulliford recited the play's clever epilogue, Rosalind, still trembling, asked Pope in the tiring room, "Did I disgrace you, master?"

"Robin, you did not." He was smiling. So were other players who came clustering to congratulate her. Even Burbage had a clap on the arm for her.

Ben Jonson came, too, as Rosalind walked about the tiring room in a daze, still in her shepherdess costume. He hit her so hard on the shoulder that he near sent her reeling into the pots of paints. "Well done, Master Robin," he roared at her. "Already folk ask your name. Who is that pretty brown shepherdess?"

"Who asked my name, Master Jonson?" Rosalind was greatly flattered. She had hoped she would be noticed by someone other than her master and the other players.

"A man who sat near to me in the gallery. He was ill-favored and swart, with burns on the back of his hands, but he spoke civilly enough. He asked me if you had played in *Henry V,* for he had seen it, too. He seemed to mark you out as a court lady in that play, though he said you stood so much behind other players that he could seldom see your face. And he thought your complexion in that play was fairer than it is now. I told him I believed you had been an attendant to the Princess of France in that play."

As Rosalind reached for a cloth to wipe the brown paint off her face, she recalled Dickon's words of a "neighbor from Cowley." This neighbor had been dark-faced and his hands had also borne scars. "Master Jonson, did he tell you who he was?"

"No, he did not. But he asked your name. I told him you were named Robin a Dale."

"Did he say he came from Oxfordshire?"

"No. He asked only who you were, where your home is, and how long you have been with the Lord Chamberlain's Company."

"Was his beard a black one?" A chill struck at Rosalind, making her shiver, though the tiring room was hot.

"Aye, a fork beard. Do you know him? I said that I scarce knew you, that you lived somewhere in London Town, not in Southwark, and that you had not been long with the company. I told him but little, though he pressed me hard enough. And I told him little of the truth." Jonson chuckled. "I thought perhaps he sought to collect a debt from you. I do not want to see you in debtor's prison or any other prison, Robin."

Rosalind was grateful. "I do not know this man, Master Jonson. But I have had some word of him before." When Jonson had left her for Burbage's company, she muttered into her looking glass, "I wish, Master Jonson, that you had told this man nothing of me at all."

VII
THE QUEEN'S COMMAND

In the summer dusk of that same day Martin Sclater left London at a gallop for the north. He rode swiftly, arriving near midnight at the brick house on the outskirts of Saint Albans. He left his horse with a yawning groom and hurried to the door to hammer on it with his fist. A maidservant opened it, candle in hand.

"Take me to Master Fenchurch," he ordered.

Adam Fenchurch was abed. When he was told by the maidservant who had come, he ordered his bed hangings drawn back and swiftly sat up. He spoke to Sclater eagerly, " 'Tis far too long since I have seen you. I was about to come to London after you. You have found the girl?"

Sclater nodded. "I think I may have. I marked out a lad again today in Southwark who I thought resembled you, though his face was brown painted, and he wore a wig of black hair. He is named Robin a Dale."

Fenchurch looked puzzled. "*Again?* Robin a Dale? A wig? I do not understand you. What are you saying?"

Sclater explained. "Robin a Dale is a player. He is with

the Lord Chamberlain's Company. Sometime ago this player took the part of a French lady at Burbage's new playhouse in Southwark. I had been searching in Southwark for some time. I did not see this boy player well the first time I came to the playhouse, but today the part the player bore was a larger one—one in which there were speeches. I heard the speeches the player made very clearly. I think it is Rosalind Broome I saw. I think she pretends still to be a boy and has now become a player of women's parts. Today she was a shepherdess and wore, as I told you, a wig of black hair. Players sometimes take other names, I hear."

"Aye, players might." Fenchurch lay back among his pillows. "Ride to London now, Martin. Tend to this matter of the shepherdess if you are certain this is the girl we seek. I will join you in a week's time at the Golden Rose in Fleet Street. My work for Sir Robert Cecil is finished here in Hertfordshire. I have the list of secret enemies of the Queen, those men in this county who speak treason in the taverns. I have the names of men who praise Lord Essex to the skies. Ride hard, Martin. Attend to the matter as swiftly as you can, and let no man see what you must do."

Weary from the excitement of the previous day and from uneasy midnight dreams of a man with scarred hands, Rosalind slept late the next morning. She awoke with a shuddering start, not to Dame Gillet's usual soft call that it was dawning, but to her master's loud shouting into her ear. Rubbing her eyes, her heart pounding with fright, she sat up in bed. To her shock, three men stood about it, Pope at its foot, Henry Condell on one side, and Burbage on the other. Condell was red with fury as she had never seen him before. Burbage was gnawing at his mustache and Pope at a fingernail. Dame Gillet stood behind the large player, her apron to her mouth in dismay.

"What is it?" asked Rosalind in alarm.

Condell exploded, "It is Gulliford! After supper last night he ran away to join the Lord Admiral's Company, our rivals. They lured him with golden promises to humble us now and leave us without a Rosalind for our play today. He will now play parts for them."

Rosalind was paralyzed with shock. Gulliford gone? What of the remaining two performances of *As You Like It?* All new plays were performed three times.

Bending over her, Burbage stabbed a sharp finger into her face. "I will never welcome Gulliford again. Condell is well rid of him. I am told you know the part of Rosalind from copying it and aiding Gulliford, curse the whelp!"

She nodded. "Aye, Master Burbage, I think I do. . . ."

"We shall find out if you do here and now and in this chamber. You shall play Rosalind to my Orlando and you, Master Pope and Master Condell, will play your parts as at the Globe. Dame Gillet, you will read all other parts." Rosalind saw Burbage take the script of the play from under his cloak and hand it to the trembling woman.

For two long hours, in her nightgown with her long robe over it and with her bare feet growing colder and colder with each line she spoke, Rosalind played the witty Rosalind of the play. When she had said the heroine's last words, " 'When . . . I make courtsey, bid me farewell,' " She went to perch exhausted on the edge of her bed.

"What think you?" asked Pope of Burbage. "Robin knows the lines well enough to please me."

The great actor was silent, frowning, for a long time. Then he said quietly and with a sigh, "He has been with us less than a year, but you and Dame Gillet have done well with him. I have no wish to stop the play. This afternoon Robin a Dale shall be Rosalind, and we shall see that we shall see. God be praised, Rosalind does not sing in the play. I have heard this lad." Burbage turned to Condell. "Your other lad, Davey, must play Phebe. You say you set him to learning Phebe's lines last night. That was clever of you. Like this boy, little Davey is quick and he is a comely lad, too. He must make do as the shepherdess today, even if he may stumble sometimes in Phebe's part. The prompter will watch him well and give him his lines."

Still talking to Condell, Burbage left, followed by Dame Gillet. When they had gone, Pope came to sit heavily beside Rosalind. "Robin, you must show all London something of your courage this afternoon. I will be honest with you. No soldier ever required more than you will need today."

Playing Rosalind that day she did not find herself in a pleasant dream as she had when she had played the shepherdess. Everything was only too frighteningly real to her now. But she knew the play well from copying cue sheets for so many players, and she knew the character of the high-spirited auburn-bewigged Rosalind, who as a boy carried at one time a cutlass and at another a boar spear. She remembered how Master Gulliford had played her and his movements, though she was aware, because she was not Gulliford, that her Rosalind would be a different heroine. She prayed hers would be half as good as his.

Her Rosalind was less sharp and more teasing than Gulliford's had been. When she said languishingly to the

play's hero, " 'To you I give myself, for I am yours,' " she
heard the ladies in the audience sigh happily as one. When
in the epilogue she offered to kiss all men and ladies present
who pleased her taste, she heard them all sigh in unison.
She finished with a very deep curtesy and stood, her head
bowed, totally alone on the center of the stage, not daring
to breathe. What would happen now? Would it be limp
dead cats for Robin a Dale, who had dared something
beyond his skill?

And then she heard it, the great burst of applause that
rang out from the groundlings and the galleries alike, and
not one mew nor one hiss nor one cat. It seemed to her that
not even one Londoner present held his silence. From the
penny stinkards in the pit came an approving pelting of
plums and pears for her to eat. From above, the richer
folk rained a small tinkling shower of silver pieces.

She was truly a player! Again and again she curtseyed.
Then as a jest she bowed as a gentleman should. After all,
they thought she was a lad. The audience roared with joy
at her wit. They laughed even more when the play's clown
in his yellow-and-russet costume, ass's ears, and cockscomb
crest bounded comically onto the stage and, scolding,
hauled her off by the arm so the other players could come
out and be applauded, too. "Good folk of London," the
clown shouted to the throng, "do you not wish to see our
jig? When I am rid of this bold wench, you shall."

One man in the audience had not applauded the play.
Martin Sclater, sitting in the gallery for the second performance of *As You Like It,* had paid little heed that
afternoon to the auburn-haired lad who played Rosalind,
though the actor's voice had at times sounded somewhat

familiar to him. He had had eyes only for the black-haired shepherdess, Phebe. Somehow, though, she seemed plumper and shorter to him than yesterday, and her voice a bit higher. But that, he told himself, was only the effect of his long exhausting search and all-night ride from Saint Albans. The words of the shepherdess and the costume had been the same as yesterday.

Sclater waited in the gallery until the throng departed, then walked outside the Globe and around it to the players' private door. There he asked the trumpeter, who had popped his head out to stare suspiciously at the now darkening sky, "Where can I find the lad who today played the black-haired shepherdess? I have a message for him from his kinsman." In Martin's palm lay a shilling.

Eager to be of help, the trumpeter told him, "In Saint Mary Aldermansbury with Master Condell, who is also a player." As if in afterthought, the trumpeter turned to gaze at the Thames. Then he pointed. "Look you, sir, the boy you seek is walking to the river now. There he is. You can catch him if you hasten. He is the fair-haired lad in the scarlet doublet and black breeches, the boy with the white feather in his hat."

"I thank ye," Martin told the trumpeter, who ducked back inside the playhouse after he had taken the shilling.

Sclater made haste. A grove of trees stood between the Globe and the river and its waiting watermen with their boats for hire. As he entered the shadow of the trees, the man's hand went to the dagger at his hip.

Master Condell came that night late to the Falcon, where the Lord Chamberlain's Company celebrated the success of *As You Like It* with a new heroine. Rosalind sat among them, happy, knowing that her Rosalind had made her a full-fledged player.

Condell's news took the edge of joy from her. His face was stark white, and he shivered as he stood before Burbage and the others. He burst out, "Who would kill my little lad, Davey? Bones o' God, Davey did no harm to any man. The shepherdess was his first part of any importance. He was so happy to have played it well he would not wait to go home with me. He set off alone to tell my wife and children his news." Blinking hard, Condell looked up into the tavern's beams. "My poor wife weeps anew. Yesterday Gulliford left us, and now the smaller lad who loved us well is dead. He was—"

"Where was he killed?" asked Burbage, sharply interrupting, getting up from the table.

In a broken voice Condell told him how the boy's body had been found under some elms by watermen after nightfall and how the watchman of the Globe, who had been sent for, had identified him. The Watch of Southwark had come and gone, claiming to be mystified. Davey had been stabbed to death, though not a farthing was taken from him.

"You say his purse was not taken?" questioned Pope. "I find that passing strange."

"Aye, it was not thieves' work that the Watch could see. A rogue would have taken Davey's knife as well. It was a gift to him from my wife and no poor trifle. It had a haft of silver."

Rosalind listened, thinking. A canting man would have stolen both purse and dagger. She wished that she had paid more heed to Condell's younger boy and that she had taken the trouble to congratulate him on his Phebe. She had been too full of herself after playing Rosalind to think of anyone but herself. And now it was too late to do anything but mourn him.

Condell sat down next to Rosalind. "The trumpeter alone of the men at the Globe had something to say of this, though he did not think it was of any importance."

"What did he say?"

"That a man asked him after the play who had played the part of the shepherdess. He had a message for that player from his kinsman."

Burbage demanded, "Did the trumpeter know this man?"

"No, he had never seen him before. He scarce looked at his face, but as the man gave him a shilling for pointing Davey out to him, the trumpeter saw his hands. They were scarred. He said further that the man was swart and fork-bearded."

"By the Tyburn Mark?" asked Pope.

"The trumpeter did not say."

Rosalind drew in her breath. Scarred hands. A man with scars on his hands had asked questions about her. Was it the same man? Had this man killed the little player? She shuddered, all pleasure gone in her triumph of the day.

Sitting at a table in a private room of the Golden Rose less than a mile from the Falcon, Martin Sclater wrote a letter to Fenchurch. It said only: "I have found Mistress Rosalind and given her your greetings."

Summer passed but Rosalind took no more lead roles in plays. Thomas Pope did not think her fully ready until

winter at the earliest. Disappointed, she had to admit that
there was merit in his words. What guarantee was there
that she could be so successful again? An experienced and
older lad from a country company was sent for by Burbage
to play parts this youth knew already, parts he had performed in older plays. The new player was more cheerful
than Gulliford had been, but at once he attached himself
to Burbage like samphire to a cliff. The very ambitious
young actor had an eye to his future when he would play
men's parts. He was near nineteen years. Soon he would
not be able to manage a woman's treble voice.

Rosalind found much to occupy her time—her work to
please Pope and Dame Gillet and her copying for Master
Will. She did these things well enough to satisfy them, but
her thoughts were no longer totally given over to becoming
a player. She found two men preying on her mind always
as she went about London Town as a boy—Tom o' Bedlam
and the mysterious, swarthy man with scarred hands. Hard
as she tried to remember, she knew no one at all in Cowley,
or for that matter in Oxford, who was like him.

At times she thought of Lord Essex, too, whom she
blessed in her prayers each night. The gossip of the city
was that he fared badly in Ireland. His army had suffered
defeats at the hands of the Irish rebels. The Queen was
not pleased with him.

Tom Pope told her one Sunday evening, "Queen Elizabeth favors peace over war, God be praised. Wars are
costly to her purse. When Lord Essex returns, she will have
something very hard to say to him for all that he is
London's favorite."

Dame Gillet, knitting nearby, looked up and smiled,
then said, "Aye, the Queen will."

Rosalind mused, looking into the flames on the hearth, "Essex must win in Ireland then? No one can win always at all times. It is not just to expect a person to win always."

The woman laughed. "You grow wise to know that, Robin. But those who serve the Queen must not fail. It is not just. But it is true."

Rosalind said with a frown, "My father died in Spain for her and for Lord Essex."

"So he did. So did many. But that is little to the Queen or Lord Essex or to the Queen's Secretary, Sir Robert Cecil," answered Dame Gillet.

"Aye, Dame Gillet has the right of it," Pope told the girl. "Pin no great hopes to Essex. You told me you spoke once to him at the Royal Exchange and told him your name and that of your father. He will have forgotten you by now. I am certain of it."

"Yes, master." His words made Rosalind sigh. She was wiser now, in fact, for her year among the players. She had seen how quickly Londoners forgot her triumph as Rosalind in the play. She must play many more parts to become so great and famous a player as Burbage or her master. No, she would not seek out the great lord again. It had been too bold of her. Perhaps he'd know someday who Robin a Dale, player, was, but that would not be Rosalind Broome who had once adored him.

"Master Pope," she said. "Lord Essex made a strange remark. He said he would trade places with me because I need fear no knife in the dark."

"Essex needs fear every other ambitious man in England; most of all he needs fear Sir Robert Cecil and the Queen," advised Pope. "But who would harm a mere player?"

Dame Gillet snorted. "Who killed Condell's small lad Davey then? And why? Was it someone escaped from Bedlam, where the madmen are kept in chains?"

"It could only have been a madman, dame," said Pope.

While the players rehearsed Ben Jonson's newly finished comedy, news of Lord Essex came fast and furious to Rosalind's ears. The earl had returned unexpectedly from Ireland. Mud-stained from his swift ride across England, he had forced his way into the Queen's private apartments. She had received him warily at first, fearing him and the armed men with him. Then, when she had more control, she changed her mind and ordered him taken in a coach to her Lord Keeper's London house, York House. By her order no man could visit him without her permission. The great and popular noble was not in the dread Tower of London but all the same under lock and key.

With others all pretending to be passersby, Rosalind went to stare at the iron gates of York House beyond which Essex was confined. The Queen's red-garbed soldiers, each armed with a halberd, stood guard there. They glared fiercely at the boys who came too near to peep between the railings into the flagstone court.

That same September Master Will's newest play, *Julius Caesar,* was produced at the Globe. In this play Rosalind once more had a part, certainly not half so good as that of Rosalind in *As You Like It.* This time she was wife to Caesar and had but few lines to speak. Burbage and Pope were well satisfied with her performance but gave her no parts in other plays. She did not ask Shakespeare again for a part in a new play he was writing. But she loved him well for the kind words he gave her when she was at the play-house with him. Master Burbage and some others were often snappish.

In November, while Lord Essex lay still at York House, the Queen's Master of Revels commanded the Lord Chamberlain's Company to Richmond Palace to play before her. The play he requested was *As You Like It*.

Rosalind waited in an agony. What would Master Burbage decide: would he choose her as Rosalind once more or assign the part to the new and more experienced boy player? This boy had learned it also, something she had resented until Pope had pointed out that it was only wise in the event of sudden illness for actors to know each other's parts. He mentioned Gulliford's name in the same breath, though he did not say that if Rosalind had not known Gulliford's part as Rosalind, there would have been no play that day. The company would have lost a good deal of money.

Richard Burbage came to Pope's house on the first of December. He supped with Pope, Rosalind, and Dame Gillet. Over the sweet cakes he told Rosalind that he had decided Robin a Dale should play Rosalind before the Queen. He asked, "Have you the stomach for this? Are you bold enough, shy Robin?"

"Aye, master, I think I can be." She laughed nervously. "The Queen does not keep dead cats to hand?"

"No, she has other ways of showing her displeasure. They are far more terrible than a dead cat, Robin," answered Pope.

"Aye, the person who displeases her might have to deal with her dwarf of a secretary," put in Dame Gillet, her mouth awry with disgust.

"Best hold your tongue, dame," warned Pope. "The walls have ears where Sir Robert is concerned."

Richmond Palace, one of the Queen's favorites, was also on the south side of the Thames some seven or eight miles from Southwark. The players were taken upriver by one of the Queen's red, blue, and gold barges and deposited on the riverbank, then brought by wagons to the palace.

When she had been a small girl Rosalind had been summoned by a Cowley farmer to see the rabbit burrow he had opened with his plow. Curious about it, she had taken a spade and unearthed more of it. The burrow had been multibranched with many entryways and exits.

As she walked beside Master Pope in her scarlet doublet, breeches, and hose, the livery of the Lord Chamberlain's Company, she thought Richmond Palace resembled the Cowley rabbit's home. It was made up of chamber after chamber, of broad and narrow stairways, and long galleries where footsteps echoed. Some chambers were heated against the winter chill by braziers of glowing coals. Others were bitterly cold. Enormous as the palace seemed to be, Rosalind thought of it as crowded. People were everywhere, smiling, nodding, and whispering as the players passed. Rosalind thought after twenty minutes of marching along, led by one of the Queen's ushers, that they would never reach the place where they were to perform.

Suddenly, however, the usher stopped in the center of a long gallery where two men stood together. The usher bowed low. Pope whispered to Rosalind, "Bow, Robin, and doff your hat. It is Sir Robert Cecil himself."

Rosalind bowed, then looked up almost afraid to see Dame Gillet's "dwarf." But Cecil was not a dwarf for all that he was tiny. He was a hunchback in a long, brown, fur-trimmed gown. His face was very pale and his hazel eyes very bright. Rosalind found his face more sad than terrible. His smile was a sweet one. Even more to her surprise, he was not at all old.

She glanced from him to the tall, black-haired man beside him. This man was dressed very finely in murrey-red velvet and gold lace. It was all she could do to keep from crying out when she looked into his face, and she drew every bit of her player's craft to compose her own. For all of his fine clothing he was surely Tom o' Bedlam! And Tom was staring directly at her as she stood between Pope and Burbage, with Master Will and Henry Condell behind her.

Sir Robert Cecil's voice was soft as he addressed Burbage, "I bid you very welcome here, Master Burbage."

Burbage bowed once more as Rosalind locked glances with Tom o'Bedlam. She heard Burbage saying, "We thank you, Sir Robert. Will you come to our play tonight?"

"Alas, I cannot find the time. I have business here with Master Compton and with others. Come this way when you have finished, and I will speak with you again."

Master Compton? Was that Tom o'Bedlam's true name? And what was he doing here at Richmond Palace?

The Queen's Secretary turned away to look out the gallery window, and Tom o' Bedlam turned with him, inclining his head toward the tiny man. This was the signal for the usher to start on his way again.

Sick with fright, Rosalind went along beside Pope, her knees pumping up and down, though she could not say how they managed to. Had Tom recognized her? Today she was garbed very richly like the others with her. Before, whenever he had seen her, she had worn only the coarse brown doublet and the breeches and hose of a country boy. Aye, she was greatly changed in costume! He had looked hard at her, but she had not seen any true light of recognition in his face. She knew there had been none on hers, at least after the first moment. She was player enough to keep her face closed.

At last the usher stopped. He took them into an antechamber, where they found a tiring man from the Globe and a chest of costumes and another of small properties for the play. The crook of the shepherdess was there as well as the boar spear Rosalind carried at times as the heroine of the play. She sat down at once on a stool, her legs shook so much. Richard Burbage took one glance at her face and spoke to Pope. "Look to your lad, Robin. He's gone stark white."

Pope came over to her, "Are you afraid, Robin?"

She nodded.

"Do you fear to play before the Queen?"

She stared up at him, wishing she could tell him of Tom o' Bedlam and the rogues, but that would mean she must reveal herself as someone the City Watch sought—and in time reveal herself as a girl. She nodded. "Aye, the Queen."

"Do not be afraid. She favors plays and players and so do her courtiers. Put your thoughts to the play, not on the Queen, and all will be aright. Now come make ready."

After Rosalind had got into her costume and painted her face for the first act of the play, the Queen's Master of Revels, a worried-looking man in a violet satin doublet, came into the antechamber wringing his hands. He spoke hurriedly to Burbage, gesturing toward a closed door, which was carved and painted with golden scrollwork. "Your players will enter through this door. I have done what I could for you in the matter of a stage." He opened his hands and laughed. "But you must remember we have little room, and it is sometimes difficult."

Shakespeare, not far from Rosalind, said in a very low voice, "The meaning of this is that the one small tree you now stand behind, shy Robin, will soon be taken out of this room and will serve as my entire Forest of Arden. We have little room at court. It is always difficult."

Her fist to her mouth, Rosalind waited, her ear to the door, until she heard her cue. Then she entered onto a small wooden platform, which was the Master of Revels' idea of a stage. Small it was, indeed!

While another player said his lines to her, Rosalind, as the heroine, looked swiftly about. Tom o' Bedlam, Lord be praised, did not seem to be there. The candle-lit chamber was not large, though it must have held near two hundred men and women. Most were standing, jammed so close together that she wondered if they could breathe at all. At one end of the room there was a space on which no one encroached. There, surrounded by white-clad maidens perched on cushions, sat Queen Elizabeth in a gilded chair.

Her knowing player's eye told Rosalind that the Queen was as painted as she was at that moment. Beneath the white and vermilion Elizabeth was old and wrinkled. Her red hair was as false as the auburn hair Rosalind now wore as a wig. The Queen's face was long, thin, and shrunken onto her cheekbones. Only her hands were still fair. Her gown was dazzling, of pearl-colored satin. Its sleeves were slashed and lined with cloth of silver. Behind her head arose a fan-shaped collar of silver lace, adorned with pearl and diamond pendants. More pearls were around her neck and entwined in her wig, and over her forehead dangled huge teardrop pearls.

Rosalind spoke her first line looking at the Queen. " 'Dear Celia, I show more mirth than I am mistress of, or would you yet I were merrier?' "

As the boy actor who played Celia replied to her, Rosalind's eyes moved once more over the throng. Had she missed seeing Tom o' Bedlam? He was tall. He would stand head and shoulders above most of the people here. No, he had not come to the play. She let out her breath in relief.

Her eyes had focused for only an instant on the tall, thin, fair-haired man who leaned against the wall to her left. He was frowning, his dark brows gathered together in a bar as he stared at her. She did not see him bring his hand to his chin and rub it thoughtfully as the play went on. She did not look at him again, though she stole glances at the Queen, who sometimes smiled at Master Will's witty lines and waved her hand keeping time to the play's songs.

VIII

MASTER ROSALIND

When Rosalind had spoken the final words of the play's epilogue, "'. . . when I make curtsey, bid me farewell,'" and curtseyed, she heard Queen Elizabeth's ringing voice. "Well done. Well done!" Then the old woman clapped her hands for a time.

Still sunk into a curtsey on the icelike stone floor, Rosalind saw how the courtiers watched the Queen. The instant after she had finished applauding, they stopped, too.

The Queen cried out, gesturing, "Send Master Burbage to me now."

Rosalind watched Burbage, who had acted the hero of *As You Like it,* walk to the Queen and go down on one knee before her. "Very well done, indeed," she told him. "You shall play before me again and very soon." She waved her hand. Burbage got up and backed away, bowing and bowing.

Next the Queen's eye fell on Rosalind and the company's three boys who had played girls that day. "Come here, come here, lads," she commanded.

By now Rosalind was almost as afraid of the Queen as of Tom o' Bedlam. For once she was happy that she wore skirts and no one could see how her knees knocked together. She came slowly to the end of the chamber with the other players, bowed, remembering she was supposed to be a boy, then sank down into another curtsey in her wide skirts of seawater-green taffeta.

Queen Elizabeth laughed and told them, "Pretty, pretty, very pretty you are, my sweet little maids in a row, though I know you are not maids at all and soon will grow fierce beards." All at once the old woman singled out Rosalind. "Boy, what are you called?"

"Robin a Dale," Rosalind said in a very small voice.

The Queen laughed at her squeak. "I've caught me a little mouse, have I not? And you spoke so saucily in the play. It is more easy to speak on the stage than to me, eh?"

Rosalind could only nod and stare up into the woman's small, almond-shaped black eyes. This was the woman who held the great Lord Essex prisoner because he had not done well in Ireland and had dared show his anger to her. Aye, her eyes were hard, hard and bright as a ferret's.

The Queen went on, "The cat has your tongue, I see. Either that or you know only the fair speeches Master Shakespeare puts into your mouth with his pen. Go back now. Perhaps the lad who played Phebe will speak with me, if he does not yawn in my face. He is so small he is awake long past his bedtime, I suspect. Go away if you cannot speak to me, Master Rosalind."

Her cheeks ablaze with humiliation, Rosalind backed away, aware of the laughter of the courtiers and the Queen's maids-in-waiting.

"Master Rosalind! Master Rosalind!" The name echoed around the chamber. One fair-haired man standing against the wall burst out laughing. Other courtiers took up his laughter at Rosalind's expense.

Rosalind was still blushing as she took off her costume in a corner of the makeshift tiring room. She had spoken with Master Pope as she'd come offstage and heard him try to comfort her. "The Queen has a hard tongue but all the same, Robin, you did not displease her. But never again let me see you watching the audience and not your fellow players. It is your fellow players you must pay heed to. Master Burbage saw you also tonight. Because this is your first time at court and you wanted to see the Queen, he will forgive you. But now you have seen her, do not do so again."

The girl had muttered in anger, "No, master. I do not want to see her again. I do not care if I have pleased her or not. I felt a fool before her."

"Aye, Robin, many men do. You are not singled out by her to play the fool any more than some others far greater than you and I."

Later when she had put on the red livery, she asked Pope, "Must we see the Queen's Secretary again?"

"We must. He asked us to return by the same gallery. I thought you would find him courteous."

"I did, master."

"But you fear him too? You have listened too much to the words of Dame Gillet concerning him."

Rosalind looked up into Pope's eyes. "Master, is the Queen's Secretary truly an enemy to Lord Essex?"

Pope bent to say softly, "He is, indeed. It is doubtful if

Essex has any greater enemy. Do you love Essex so much still?"

Rosalind shook her head as the Queen's usher hurried up, bowed, and started the players on their way out of Richmond Palace. No, Essex sought popularity with all Londoners. She'd learned from going about the city of his arrogance and that he accepted the love of anyone who would support his cause. Walking beside Pope once more, she asked, "Why are they enemies?"

"Because the Queen and her Secretary believe that Lord Essex wishes to make himself the ruler of England."

Rosalind recalled the comment that she had overheard the day the Queen had returned to London. "I heard a man say Essex should share her throne. He is young and strong. She is old."

"She is old—and strong. She will never share her throne with anyone, Robin."

As they neared the gallery Rosalind bit her lip, hoping that Tom o' Bedlam would be gone away by now. They had played for more than two hours. She put him out of her mind with an effort and thought of the Queen. A terrible old woman Elizabeth was, a woman with a witch's face under entangled pearls atop a red wig.

To Rosalind's great relief Tom o' Bedlam was not with Sir Robert Cecil. Another man had taken his place, one who was far more to Rosalind's liking if only because he was a stranger to her. This man was attractive, tall, with yellow hair a little darker than hers, and with eyes as dark, though whether they were deep blue or brown like hers she could not tell. The gallery was dimly lit by candles in sconces. The man's brows were very dark, contrasting strangely with his fair hair. Compared to Tom o' Bedlam's his clothing was somber—gray satin doublet with black breeches and hose.

The usher stopped before the little Secretary and the stranger and bowed. "I have brought the players again to you, Sir Robert."

"As I see." The Secretary addressed Burbage, "I regret, sir, that I did not see your play tonight. Master Fenchurch here tells me it pleased everyone very well."

"I thank you, Sir Robert."

The hunchback went on, "You played the hero I am told, Master Burbage. Master Fenchurch says that the lad who played Rosalind enchanted all who heard him as all were enchanted by you."

"Robin," Burbage ordered, "come here."

Not so frightened now that Tom o' Bedlam was gone, Rosalind came forward and bowed to the two men.

"Is this the lad?" she heard Sir Robert ask Fenchurch.

"Aye, this is the Rosalind."

Burbage explained, smiling. "Robin a Dale is his name."

Fenchurch was smiling, too. "I shall think of him as Rosalind." He paused, staring at her. "I was in Saint Albans at the time this play was first performed, so I could not know for certain. Wasn't a player of the name of Robin who played in it murdered last summer in Southwark? I believe I heard a ballad sung of him. He was stabbed, was he not?"

As spokesmen of the players massed standing behind him, Burbage said, "This is Robin a Dale, our only Robin. There was a boy player murdered, sir. His name was Davey. There is no ballad of him that I have heard."

The Queen's Secretary nodded, then put in, "I have not heard such a ballad either. I listen well to ballads. They give me the news of London." He spoke to Rosalind. "Young master, your face interests folk tonight. The man who was with me earlier asked me of you. He wanted to know who you are and where you live. I told him I did not know you. Now I know who you are, but I still do not know where you live."

To Rosalind's helpless terror, Burbage stated, "Why, in Southwark with Master Pope here. Robin is his apprentice."

Sir Robert nodded once more. "So? If anyone should ask me again of Robin a Dale, the player, I shall tell him these things. Good night to you, Master Burbage and Master Robin."

"Master Rosalind," Fenchurch corrected, chuckling.

As the players went down the gallery in a body, Rosalind's heart pounded with fright once more. So Tom o' Bedlam had asked about her. Did that mean he had recognized her?

Sir Robert Cecil turned his attention to Adam Fenchurch. "What brings you here tonight? I did not send for you. Do you have something to tell me?"

"No, Sir Robert, I but came to see the play and hoped to find you and ask you of my uncle's barony of Broome. I claimed it of the college of heralds months past but find it takes them tedious long to verify me as Lord Broome."

The Secretary looked out the gallery window in front of him into the absolute darkness of Richmond Park. He said, "When I have news of this, I shall summon you. Her Maj-

esty's heralds work very slowly. Do not be impatient."
He gazed up at the tall man. "That player, the boy, resembled you greatly. Did you notice? He could have been
kin to you—the boy you named Master Rosalind."

"I did not notice, Sir Robert. And it was not I who
named him that. It was the Queen. He played a girl by the
name of Rosalind tonight. When the Queen spoke to him,
he could only squeak at her, he was so frightened. He
could not speak out as a man, so she called him by a girl's
name."

"Poor boy," said the Secretary.

Four chambers and another gallery away from Cecil and
Fenchurch, Pope said softly to Rosalind, "How like you
are to the man we saw with Sir Robert. Did you notice the
resemblance, Robin?"

"No, master." Rosalind had Tom o' Bedlam too much
on her mind to concentrate on the man named Fenchurch.
Did Tom know who she was? What did he feel toward her
now that more than a year had passed? She must know.
Moll would know, and Moll could advise her. That is, if
Moll would keep her promise to her. No, Rosalind decided, she would not go to the dancing master tomorrow
morning. She would go to the rogues' tavern in Billingsgate looking for Moll or for the Upright Man of London.

She heard Pope's words to Burbage. "Did you see how
much our Robin was like unto the man with Sir Robert?"

"I marked it well, Master Pope. Is this Fenchurch kin to
you, Robin? An uncle or a cousin?"

"No, Master Burbage," Rosalind told him, "I have no
cousins or uncles that I know, unless they are in Sussex.
But they would be named Broome, not Fenchurch."

"Broome? There are noble lords by that name," came from Burbage. "I had not thought of this before, though you told me your name was Broome, as I recall."

Rosalind said dully, "I know them not, Master Burbage. I have never gone to Sussex."

At midnight Martin Sclater awoke in his small chamber in the Golden Rose to cry out at the scalding drip of candle tallow falling on his face. His master, his mouth twisted with fury, was bending over his bed, candle in hand. "Martin, you killed the wrong boy last summer," he said through his teeth. "That boy you killed was not Robin a Dale. Rosalind Broome, or Robin a Dale, as she calls herself, is the apprentice of the player, Thomas Pope. I saw them both this very night at Richmond Palace where they played before the Queen. The girl lives in Pope's house in Southwark."

"Do you wish me to kill the girl still, master?" asked Sclater.

Grunting, Fenchurch jammed the candle down into a holder next to Martin's bed. "How else am I to have my barony? Do it with care and in secret, but do not delay overlong. Learn the girl's habits first. I want no question as to her death. She is a player and known to many folk now by name. Be clever, Martin."

Rosalind went over London Bridge the next morning with an empty basket on her arm. She'd promised Dame Gillet to go to Billingsgate after she'd visited the dancing master and there buy eels and whiting for supper. She disliked lying about attending her dancing lesson, but at least she would go to the fish market. Before that she'd visit the Gun, hoping she might find Moll there.

The first person Rosalind recognized when she came into the common room of the Gun was Dickon, the nip. The jostler was not with him, which made her wonder. Dickon sat on the edge of a table, swinging his legs. Behind him at a distance sat the Upright Man deep in conversation with an elegantly garbed highwayman Rosalind knew from an earlier meeting. Dickon came to her at once and peered hopefully into her basket, then stared at her purse. She opened it and gave him two pennies.

"Where can I find Moll, Dickon?"

"At Smart's Quay."

"Where is the jostler?"

"Sick abed at Moll's house wi' a fever."

"Dickon, I want to talk with the Upright Man. Will you ask him for me?"

"Na, I be next to talk to him, Rosalind."

She opened her purse again and gave him a groat. "If it please you, Dickon, I haven't much time and have no more money to give you. I must buy fish for my mistress."

"I'll ask him." Dickon went to the Upright Man and whispered into his ear, then pointed at Rosalind. The leader of the rogues first scowled at her, then laughed as she took off her hat to be recognized. He beckoned with a finger.

When she was seated by him and the highwayman, he asked, "How does it fare with ye, girl?"

Rapidly she told the rogue of her new identity as a player in the Lord Chamberlain's Company while Dickon and the highwayman listened.

The Upright Man sounded very surprised. "Ye've gulled great Master Burbage into thinking ye be a lad?"

The highwayman laughed. "She must be a player, indeed."

Rosalind told him, "I thank you. I always wished to be a boy."

"You carry yourself well as a boy," was the compliment from the highwayman. "I have heard of Robin a Dale."

Rosalind turned to the Upright Man. "I am troubled. I'd hoped to see Moll. Will you help me?"

"As I baptized ye, I shall."

"The Lord Chamberlain's Company played before the Queen last night at Richmond Palace. I saw Tom o' Bedlam there in company with the Queen's Secretary."

The Upright Man asked solemnly, "Did ye see him?"

"Sir Robert Cecil called him Master Compton."

"Aye, I know that. It is a name Tom sometimes uses."

"I think Tom knew my face. He asked Sir Robert where I lived, but Sir Robert did not know so could not tell him." She paused. "Does Tom o' Bedlam seek to kill me?"

"*Kill ye?*"

"Aye, he said once he would strangle me as he'd strangle a cat that clawed him." Rosalind bit her lip. She'd thought half the night of the death of small Davey, who had also played Phebe. There could have been a man with scarred hands involved in Davey's death. The trumpeter at the Globe seemed to think so. She told the rogues now of the murder of the boy player and of the man with scars on his hands. Then she looked into the nip's face. "Tell them, Dickon, of the swart man who asked you and the jostler about a lad or a maid from Cowley."

Dickon snapped his fingers. "Aye, I remember. 'Twas in Saint Paul's Church such a man come up to us. He give me but a groat and said he was from Cowley and searchin' for a lad or wench named Broome."

Rosalind nodded. "The man who killed Davey said he had a message from his kin." She took a deep breath and asked the Upright Man directly, "Sir, would Tom o' Bedlam hire a man to kill me?"

The Upright Man's face darkened. He rubbed his chin with his hand, looking at the ceiling of the Gun. "Tom is a strange, fierce man, God knows, but it would not be in his manner to hire someone to do murder for him."

Dickon put in, "Upright Man, we didn't know the man with scarred hands. We know all the canting men in the city."

The leader of the rogues nodded agreement. "So ye do, Dickon. And so do I, or I would not be the Upright Man of London. I do not know this man. I will inquire of him."

"What of Tom?" asked Rosalind.

"I will inquire of Tom also. I had not known he'd come back to London. When he comes here, I'll ask him of ye."

Rosalind shivered. "I pray he does not mean to kill me. I never harmed him or meant to gull him."

The Upright Man shook his head. "I do not think Tom does. If he does, he will tell me."

"Could you stop him?"

"Perhaps. I understand his temper. Remember, girl, each of us serves the Devil in his way. I will ask Tom if this is the Devil's business. But I do not think it is. When I have learned something, I will send Dickon to you. I do not understand this. Perhaps it is rogue's business, but if so I was not told of it."

"And yer the Upright Man o' London," crowed Dickon.

"I am that. It is my business to know the business of canting men. Now, girl, be wary. Do not go about London or Southwark alone. You will be safest in the company of others." He spoke to the musk-scented highwayman, "Philip, do ye ply the roads south of the Thames now?"

"Aye, Upright Man."

"Then carry the girl behind ye on your prauncer safe over London Bridge to her house in Southwark."

Holding up the basket, Rosalind told him, "I must buy some fish yet." She eyed the highwayman's fine scarlet cloak doubtfully.

She heard him sigh. "Keep your basket far from me. Cock's bones, I want no stink of fish about me, though I do not object at all to having a pretty maid embrace me— even though she dresses as a lad."

Later that same day Martin Sclater sat himself down at a table in a Southwark tavern. After the potboy had brought him a cup of wine, he asked him, "Do players come here, lad?"

The potboy nodded, then went to the fire, where the innkeeper sat talking with other patrons, and spoke to him. The innkeeper got up and came over to Sclater's table. He answered the question, "Aye, master. Players come here often as do the keepers of the bears and dogs at the Bear Garden. My wine is good but cheap."

"Do you know a Master Thomas Pope?"

The innkeeper's face brightened. "Master Pope? I know him very well. All here in Southwark know him and Dame Gillet Willingson. He comes here sometimes. He is ever welcome."

After Sclater had drained his cup and put down another coin for a second, he asked, "Does a young lad come with him? A fair-haired boy, another player?"

The innkeeper shook his head. "Master Pope has had many lads live in his house. I do not know which lad you mean. He has made players of them. When they grow to manhood, they leave him. He has never wed. I think his lads serve as his sons, though in time all leave him as true sons leave their fathers."

"Where is Pope's house?"

The innkeeper named the lane.

"Who lives in the house with Pope?" asked Sclater.

"Not many folk. Master Pope's servingman and stable lad and some maids, besides Dame Gillet, who is his cook and housekeeper. Master Pope does not require many servants. He is not a great lord. He is but a player though a very prosperous one. All Southwark takes pride that he lives here, not in London Town."

"Is Pope's servingman old and feeble?"

The innkeeper chuckled. "Old and feeble? God's wounds, no. He comes here at times. He is stronger than any ox. Did you hope to take service with Master Pope?"

"Perhaps. I thought he might have need of a man to guard his house."

"Not he. Have you not seen him in certain plays? These players are marvels. I have seen Thomas Pope prick a pig's bladder sewed into another player's doublet so neatly with his sword that he does not touch the player's skin at all. The pig's blood flows out over all the stage as the other player falls dead of his sword wound. Master Pope is a deadly swordsman. Many players are. For myself, I would not play at swords or daggers with any man of the players' companies."

"Thank you for your advice," Sclater said after a pause. He laughed. "I will bear in mind what you say. I will never seek to cross a blade with Master Pope or any other player."

When the innkeeper had gone to greet a newcomer and conduct him to the fire, Sclater muttered to himself as he looked into his wine cup, "So large Thomas Pope is a master of the blade. And the man he keeps to serve him is a strong young man. I will not go to Pope's house. I must find the girl alone or in the company of someone less accomplished than Pope or one of the other players. I will tell Master Fenchurch that I must bide my time." He sighed. "He will not receive this news from me with pleasure."

Aye, Fenchurch paid well for the sort of services Martin provided, not the kind that every servingman would do. All the same Fenchurch was a hard master, but then Martin had to admit that Fenchurch also served a hard master. It was not easy to serve the Devil. It was even more difficult to please him, though he, too, paid well for services rendered.

IX

WINDSOR

Rosalind harkened to the advice of the Upright Man. She attached herself to one or the other of the players and went nowhere without them or even in Southwark without the young servingman Peter in attendance.

Thomas Pope noticed her sudden caution, and one night asked her, "Why is it, Robin, that you insist Peter go with you to the fencing master and dancing master now?"

When Rosalind hesitated, searching in her mind for a good reply, Dame Gillet came to her rescue. "Master Thomas, Robin shows wisdom. God knows, London is a parlous place. I do not go willingly over London Bridge into the city without Peter or one of the maids. London is infested with cutpurses." She stabbed a knitting needle playfully at him. "You have a sword. Robin, God be praised, does not have one as yet. As for a poor woman like me, what protection have I from rogues?"

"You have a ready tongue, Dame Gillet."

"Tut, Master Pope, a tongue does not turn away steel." She stared gravely at Rosalind. "I think that you remember well the death of small Davey."

"Aye."

"Then be wise, Robin. Go about in company if it makes you more at ease," Pope agreed. "The day will come when you will have a sword."

"And then, God's wounds, poor small Robin must fear all men," Mistress Willingson said tartly.

The nip came to Pope's house in Southwark late in January, 1600. Bold as could be, he came to the door bringing a basket of periwinkles from Billingsgate market as if he were a fishmonger. Knowing him, Rosalind suspected he had stolen the periwinkles and had watched the actor's house for a time, making sure that she was there but not the player and his housekeeper. Pope and Dame Gillet had gone over London Bridge to the christening of a player's newborn baby. Only Pope's servants and Rosalind were at home.

She took Dickon into the kitchen, where she bought his periwinkles, and then drew him into a corner so they wouldn't be overheard by the maid who was readying bread dough for the ovens.

"Did you come from the Upright Man?" she asked.

"Na, from Moll. She's talked wi' him of ya. She bids ya come ter the Gun tomorrow. Can ye come?"

Rosalind caught her lip in her lower teeth. How could she rid herself of Pope's servingman? Peter was slow-witted but still he would know the sort of tavern the Gun was. "Dickon, is there news of Tom o' Bedlam or of the man with scarred hands?"

The boy shook his head. "Not that I been told. But Moll asks ye to come. Come at midday, and Moll will be there."

At midday Rosalind went to Billingsgate having left Peter in Fleet Street absorbed in a street puppet show. It had been easy to slip away from him. And later it would be easy to tell him that she had lost sight of him in the throng and had made her way back to Southwark alone— as today she must.

To her horror, Moll and the Upright Man were not alone at the choice table by the fire. Tom o' Bedlam sat across from them, dressed once more in his rags. He looked up from his ale as she stopped dead still and stared at him. He grinned at her and spoke first. "I marked you out at Richmond Palace, and now I mark you out again."

"Master Compton, I mean you no harm," stammered the girl.

"And I mean *you* no harm," he growled. He laughed. "Who'd seek to kill *you?* Not I."

So relieved that she felt dizzy, Rosalind sat down next to laughing Moll. She told Tom, "A dark man with a forked beard and scars on his hands asks about me. Such a man murdered a small player at the Globe."

"Why would anyone kill a player?" asked Tom.

Rosalind shook her head. "No one knows. His purse and dagger were not stolen."

Tom grunted. "Not the work of a rogue then." He let out his breath in a froth of ale. "Who was this lad?"

Rosalind told him of the stabbing and of the role in the play Davey had taken and added, "The player could have been mistaken for me. The Globe's trumpeter saw the man who asked about him. He told of the man's face—swart and fork-bearded."

She saw Tom look perplexed at Moll and the Upright Man. Then after a shrug, Tom asked her, "Tell me of you. Again what is your name—your true name?"

"Rosalind Broome, of Cowley in Oxfordshire. I am called Robin a Dale here in London. Did the Queen's Secretary tell you that I live in Southwark with Pope, the player?"

Tom lifted a ragged black eyebrow. "Sir Robert?"

"Aye, Master Burbage and I talked to him two times that night at Richmond Palace."

Tom was interested in this information. "I did not see him again that night. Tell me of your family."

"I have no one but an old grandfather, who is a pastor in Cowley. He has an older brother who lives in Sussex. I have never seen him and know nothing of his family."

Tom turned his head toward the Upright Man. "Broome would be his name also then. A noble lord of that name died not long past, and it was in Sussex that he died."

The Upright Man said, "The name of Broome is not so uncommon in England."

"No, it is not," agreed Tom.

Rosalind volunteered, "The dark man who asks of me told Dickon that he came from Cowley. I know all folk in Cowley; it is so small. There is no man there like him."

"And no man among the rogues," came from Moll.

Tom nodded thoughtfully. "I go soon to Oxfordshire on my travels. I think I shall visit Cowley."

"Go to Cowley, Tom," said the leader of the rogues.

"I shall. I shall make this business my business." Tom slapped the inn table with both palms. "This swart man whoever he may be has meddled in my affairs. So I will meddle in his."

"I thank you." Rosalind beamed at the terrible Abraham Man, something she never would have believed possible.

As Rosalind got up to leave, Moll warned her, "Take care how you go about."

"My lady, I go about always with players or with Master Pope's serving man."

"Where is he now?"

"In Fleet Street, my lady, looking for me."

Moll signaled to a tall middle-aged rogue across the room. She ordered him to go with Rosalind to Fleet Street. "Do not leave her side until she has found this servingman." She addressed Rosalind directly. "Dickon or the jostler will come to you when Tom has returned from the country."

In February Will Kemp, the small clown of the Lord Chamberlain's Men, left the company of players. As the result of a wager, Kemp had announced that he would dance from London to the town of Norwich. He would start with a tabor player from in front of the Lord Mayor of London's house at seven in the morning. Rosalind went with her master and three other adult players to see Kemp start out on his madcap enterprise. She stood between Pope and another player, shouting and waving with hundreds of Londoners as popular Kemp pranced away.

She did not take note of the man who had the hood to his cloak pulled over his face as if to protect it from the knifelike February wind. She did not see how he kept his eyes on her, not on Will Kemp, and how he left the throng immediately after she and the players had turned away. Talking with Pope, she was not aware that the hooded man followed her to the north end of London Bridge.

February passed, then March. In those weeks Rosalind

saw the nip but once for a few hurried moments of conversation when she paused in Fleet Street to ask him about
Tom o' Bedlam.

He told her out of the servingman's hearing, "Tom's not
come back. Moll says some country constable has him in
prison. Tom's often there."

Very early in April Rosalind had an excellent part in a
play, this time another of Master Ben Jonson's. She sought
out Jonson's company often now. No man would come at
her with a dagger in his fierce presence. At times it still
seemed to her that he should be among the canting men,
not among players. She knew that Dame Gillet disapproved
of her friendship with Jonson, though she liked gentle Master Will Shakespeare very well. On the other hand, Pope
liked Jonson and thought very highly of his comedies.

On the second day of the performance of Jonson's play,
Rosalind came offstage when she had finished speaking her
final lines to find him in the tiring room. She bowed to him.
"Did I please you today?"

"You did, shy Robin." Jonson waved her away with a
bellowing laugh. "Shift your clothing and come back. We
must speak again."

Rosalind went among the properties outside the tiring
room. By now the players and tiring men no longer laughed
at her "silly modesty" or chided her for it. Pope had told
them over and over again, "Consider, Robin is a pastor's
grandson."

Today while she pulled off her wig among the bay trees,
she heard someone calling softly, "Rosalind. Rosalind
Broome."

"Who is it? Is it you, Dickon?" Hoping that it was the

nip, Rosalind came forward with her stiff gold brocade skirts rustling.

She could see no one. But it would be like the nip or jostler to hide behind the great bed of state and leap out at her. They could easily have come through the players' door into the properties. The door was not guarded.

"Dickon, Dickon," she called out softly, not wanting anyone in the tiring room to hear her and find the little rogue with her.

As she approached the head of the enormous bed, a man sprang from behind it, a dagger glinting in his hand.

When Martin Sclater lunged forward at her, Rosalind dived sideways, falling onto the bed. She rolled across it in a golden flurry of skirts, all the while shrieking, "Master Jonson! Master Jonson!"

Sclater dashed around the bed to catch her as she hiked up her skirts to leap a mass of stacked shields and run. She cried out again, blundering into the artificial bay trees, which being of light weight came toppling down around her. She ran into the arms of Jonson, who stood with naked sword in hand, shouting, "What is it, Robin?"

The playwright spoke but once. At his first glimpse of Sclater he pushed Rosalind aside so roughly that she fell to the floor. On her hands and knees she watched Sclater dodging about among the tombs, shields, and toppled bays. She saw him reach the door and fling it open. At that very moment Jonson caught up with him. The point of his blade plunged into Sclater's arm through the mantle he wore. As the girl got to her feet, she saw her attacker wrench free and run out the open door. Jonson didn't chase after him. He stood at the door for a long moment, then returned to Rosalind.

"There was a horse tied outside, waiting for him." He lifted the girl's trembling chin. "Do not be afraid, Robin. God's blood, no wonder you play a maiden so well. You shriek loud as any girl who has seen a ghost. 'Twas only a rogue seeking to rob you." He touched the rope of gold about her neck, part of her costume. "The rogue came to thieve among the properties, saw you here, and thought this to be real gold, which any player would know it is not."

"Aye," she told him in her fear. "He came here for somewhat." She had had only a glimpse of the man. But he had been swarthy with a forked black beard. She had not seen his hands, only what he held in one of them.

"Do not shudder so, Robin," Jonson told her. "The rogue is gone. I warrant you he'll not come back."

By now a tiring man and two players had come out, attracted by the shrieking and shouting. Jonson called to them, " 'Twas only a thief. He frightened shy Robin."

"I thought of Davey, master," Rosalind said.

Jonson's face changed. "Aye, I had forgot him. This thief will have good cause to remember Ben Jonson, though." Rosalind's glance followed Jonson's to the red-stained tip of his sword.

Sword wounds were commonplace in London. Martin Sclater found a physician not far from the Golden Rose. He washed Sclater's arm with wine, smeared a black paste over it, and bound it for him. The physician warned, "You will have little use of your arm for some weeks. The point of the blade did not touch the bone. For that you should be thankful."

Sclater only grunted. "I would be more thankful if my arm did not pain me so."

Adam Fenchurch came to the Golden Rose that night after Sclater had dispatched a potboy to him at his lodgings at another, and better, London inn. Fenchurch found his servingman lying on his bed looking at the dirty, ragged bottom of the canopy.

"Is the girl dead?" were Fenchurch's first words.

"No, she is not. I do not think I can get at her, master. She goes about always now with others. When she is not with the players, she is with Pope's servingman. He is very large. I could not approach her when Kemp danced off to Norwich. I went today to the playhouse in Southwark and came at her there, but a man ran to her rescue with a sword." Sclater got up and swung his legs over the bed, groaning. Then he said, "The man gave me this wound in the arm. If I had not had a horse ready outside the theater, he would have followed and killed me."

Fenchurch demanded, "Martin, do you think she guesses someone seeks to kill her?"

"I think so. I do not understand how she could guess this. She will be doubly wary now that I have been to the theater."

"Did she see your face?"

"Aye, she did. So did the man with the sword. I do not know if she saw my hands and the marks of burns on them I got from falling into a hearth when I was a child."

Fenchurch scowled. After a long pause he said, "Martin, I have no further use for you here in London. Go to my house in Saint Albans. Stay there until I send for you. When I have the barony of Broome, you shall come to me at the manor house in Sussex. I will not forget your services. There you will be my bailiff."

"What of the girl Rosalind, master?"

"As to her, it seems that I must deal with her in another way. So be it, Martin. I shall do so—and soon."

Still benumbed with fright, Rosalind went to Saint Paul's Church with Pope's servingman the next morning after her dancing lesson. She had said never a word of her suspicions to Pope or Dame Gillet, who accepted Ben Jonson's theory of a thief. If she told them what she believed, they might think she'd gone mad. As she'd prayed in the night that she would, she found Dickon and the jostler standing near a tomb watching for someone to pass by with a heavy purse. Leaving the servingman examining some knives for sale on another tomb now serving as a merchant's counter, Rosalind went up to the small rogues.

She told Dickon, "Tell Moll and the Upright Man that a man tried to stab me in the playhouse yesterday."

Dickon's eyes narrowed. "The man wi' the scars on his hands and black forked beard? The swart man?"

"Aye, Dickon. I think it was the same man. Has Tom o' Bedlam returned yet?"

"Na, he's still about somewheres in the country on his Devil's errands."

Rosalind gnawed at a thumbnail, then gestured toward Pope's servingman. "I cannot come to the Gun again. I must keep him near me now, Dickon. You will have to come to me in Southwark."

"Aye, Rosalind, I'll come wi' periwinkles when Tom returns."

In mid-April Queen Elizabeth, who moved from royal palace to palace outside the city, took up residence for a time at Windsor Castle on the south bank of the Thames. Her Master of Revels came once more to Richard Burbage to command a play be performed before her. The play he requested was one of Shakespeare's newest, *The Merry Wives of Windsor*. He expected the Queen to delight in it. She had often said that she was well pleased with Shakespeare's comical character, Sir John Falstaff, who had appeared in an earlier play. She wanted to see Falstaff in another play and in particular to watch "Falstaff in love."

Thomas Pope was to play the fat blustering knight Falstaff while Burbage played Master Ford. There were several parts for boy players in the new play. Rosalind was assigned the part of Mistress Page, a witty, clever wife. It was a good part and one in which she did not sing at all. In the company of other players Rosalind was not so much afraid. In Windsor, some leagues from London, she would not be afraid at all, she told herself.

The Lord Chamberlain's Company went by barge up the winding Thames to Windsor. The castle was an old stone one set on a bluff, overlooking a great green park where red deer wandered about. Beside the castle was a high, gray, stone watchtower. She longed to climb to its top, as the boy players with her also yearned. But there was no time for that. The journey by royal barge had been a long one. The properties and tiring men and Queen's Master of Revels awaited the players.

That night as the lively, scheming Mistress Page, Rosalind kept her eyes off the Queen after only a brief glance. The Queen wore a gown of white, embroidered with gold and silver thread. Because she had been likened to the moon by so many poets seeking her favor, Elizabeth played the part, garbing herself chiefly in white and moonlike colors, Rosalind had been told by Dame Gillet.

Beside her, totally eclipsed by her white radiance, stood her tiny Secretary in a long gray gown and small white ruff.

The old Queen liked the play. Even in the crowded chamber where it was played, her laughter rang out over that of others. She applauded when Pope as foolish old Falstaff was secreted in a basket and covered with dirty linen by the merry wives of the play. When the play ended and Falstaff had received his comeuppance, the Queen cried out, "Well played! Well played!" as she applauded again.

Rosalind was left to bow with eight other players, one of them Master Burbage, another Master Pope. As before, the Queen summoned the players to her. Pope and Burbage went up together to be congratulated, then the other adult actors, leaving two boy players and Rosalind standing in their wide skirts.

Queen Elizabeth beckoned them forward, too. This time Rosalind was determined not to squeak before the fierce old woman if she were spoken to.

The boy players bowed, then gave their names one by one to the Queen. Finally she turned her black gaze on Rosalind. "How now, who are you, lad?"

"Robin a Dale."

"I have seen you play before, have I not?"

"Aye, Your Majesty."

"In what play?"

" In *As You Like It* at Richmond Palace in the winter."

The old woman pointed a very long white finger at her. "Ah, you were Rosalind in that play." She laughed. "I named you Master Rosalind, did I not? Now you can speak to me. My mouse had found his voice."

Rosalind felt the blush coming to her face again. "Aye, Your Majesty." She began to back away from the Queen, but a sudden stirring in the crowd around the old woman made her stop.

The tall fair-haired man she'd seen conferring in the gallery at Richmond Palace with Sir Robert Cecil had come out of the crowd to go down on one knee before the Queen.

The old woman cried "What's this?"

At her cry, her guard of halberdiers came menacingly from their stations at the doors, their halberds pointed forward at the man.

"Hear me, Your Majesty," said Adam Fenchurch. He arose, spun around, and gestured toward Rosalind. "This player before you is a common criminal. She has stolen a book of great value from the Master of Corpus Christi College in Oxford and fled to London with it."

Frozen with shock, Rosalind heard Burbage yell from behind her, *"She?"* and heard the scrape of his shoes as he came forward.

"Aye, Master Burbage," were Fenchurch's very loud words. *"She* is not Robin a Dale or even Master Rosalind, though Rosalind is her true name. This girl is Rosalind Broome, of Cowley in Oxfordshire—and a thief."

X

THE TOWER

For what seemed to Rosalind a very long period of time there was absolute silence in the chamber while everyone looked at her in horror. The Queen's mouth was sagging open in an *O* of shocked astonishment.

Only her Secretary Sir Robert Cecil was in full control of himself. He stepped out from beside the Queen's chair and said into the stillness, "I wish to see you, Master Fenchurch, in my closet at once." The tiny man gestured toward the players but spoke to the guard. "Bring Master Burbage and the player Robin a Dale to my antechamber and keep them there." Cecil hesitated for an instant and added, "And Master Pope as well."

Then he bowed to the Queen and, backing away from her, turned about to go swiftly out of the room. Rosalind watched Fenchurch also bow, then hurry out the side door that the guards had flung open for the Secretary.

Tall red-doubleted men, the Queen's guards, came out onto the open area where the players were gathered. Their chief seemed to know Burbage and Pope. The two players were at once surrounded. Two more guards came to station themselves, one on each side of Rosalind. Without saying a word, only curtseying, she went out of the room behind the two actors and their escort.

As she walked she tried to pull her wits together but could not. All she could manage was to ask herself how the stranger Fenchurch had known she was a girl? Was he a canting man? If he were, she had never seen him. How had he known about the stolen book? Was he from Oxfordshire, too? But she had never seen him in Cowley or Oxford.

They did not go far this time through rooms and galleries. They stopped before long in a large wood-paneled room with doors at each end and one in the center. There were two window seats along one wall overlooking the deer park. The guards permitted Rosalind to sit down in one, her knees trembled so. While Richard Burbage stood in the middle of the antechamber, cracking his knuckles and sometimes stabbing Rosalind with a look of fury, Pope asked the chief of the guard, "May I speak to Robin?"

"It has not been forbidden," said the guard.

Pope sat down heavily beside Rosalind. He sighed and asked her, "Is it true? Are you a maiden?"

Rosalind nodded in misery. "Aye, Master Pope."

"Then you played at being a lad?"

She nodded again.

He sighed more deeply. "You carried yourself very well as a boy. Why did you do this? Why did you claim to be a lad?"

"To be a player. I would have chosen to be born a lad."

"You know that it is forbidden for women to play upon the stage?"

"I know, Master Pope."

The center door opened, and Adam Fenchurch came out. He did not look at the two players or at Rosalind. Smiling, he strode out of the chamber past them and the guards.

"Master Burbage," came Cecil's voice from inside the closet where he gave audiences. After another glance of anger at her, Burbage went inside, and the door was shut behind him by a guard.

Pope asked the girl, "What of this book you are said to have stolen?"

Close to tears, Rosalind told him, "I did not steal it. An Abraham Man caught me with it on the road from Oxford to Cowley. He stole it from me and brought me with him to London."

"Why did you have the book?"

"I carried it from Dr. Hornsby, the Master of Corpus Christi College, who is a friend to my grandfather. The Abraham Man thought me to be a boy. I wore boy's garb. I wore it as often as I could. It was safer for me to travel about the country in doublet and hose than in petticoats."

Pope nodded. "That would be true." He asked, "Do you know the man who accuses you?"

"No, Master Pope. I have seen him but once before—at Richmond Palace. You were with me then."

"Yes, I remember. He stood with Sir Robert at a window."

"Aye." Rosalind did not tell the actor that they had seen Tom o' Bedlam earlier that same evening and that he was the very Abraham Man who had stolen the book from her. He would think she was a liar or as mad as Tom o' Bedlam had pretended to be. She sniffled. They were both "playing," she thought, Tom and herself. She at being a lad, he at being moonstruck.

Pope fell silent, as silent as Rosalind, who held a handkerchief to her face. As she put it down and stared at the vermilion and white paint now staining it, Master Burbage came quickly out of the Secretary's chamber. He pointed at Pope and said while he mopped his forehead, "Tom Pope, Sir Robert wishes to see you now." The great actor glared once again at Rosalind and went to stand against a wall, staring up at the beams. Light from wall candles in a tall sconce shone on his painted face. Rosalind saw how the muscles of his jaw tightened as Pope passed him going inside. Suddenly Rosalind was even more frightened, not only for herself but for her master.

He was closeted with the Queen's Secretary for a longer period of time than either Fenchurch or Burbage. When he came out at last, Rosalind saw with a pang how weary he looked. He said nothing to her but came to kiss her on the forehead. She knew the kiss to be two things—a blessing and a farewell. No, she would probably not be going back to Southwark with him. She watched Burbage and Pope leave the antechamber together, passing by the guards. With all her heart she wished she could go with them as Robin a Dale.

But she was no longer Robin, the player.

At this moment the Queen's Secretary appeared in the doorway. He looked at her and crooked his finger. She got up and, walking as steadily as she could, went into his closet. It was also wood-paneled but tiny, furnished only with a table littered with papers, a chair, and a stool. He sat in the chair but did not gesture toward the stool, so she stood.

"Who are you in truth?" he demanded.

"Rosalind Broome, of Cowley in Oxfordshire."

"And you are a maiden?"

"Aye, Sir Robert."

He let out his breath in exasperation. "And you stole a book of Dr. Hornsby?"

"*I did not!*"

"But the book was stolen?"

"Yes."

"If not by you, then by whom?"

"A man who named himself Tom o' Bedlam."

"Tom o' Bedlam?" Cecil's finely shaped eyebrows lifted.

"Aye, Sir Robert, he was an Abraham Man."

"Was?"

Rosalind bit her lip. "He played at being a madman. He was not."

"And where is Tom o' Bedlam now?"

"I know not." It would not to do tell him that she had seen Tom o' Bedlam with him at Richmond Palace. He would not believe her. Besides, Tom had said he would try to help her. Saying that he was Master Compton could make him hunted. What's more, Rosalind had no idea where Tom was at the moment.

"So?" The Queen's Secretary coughed. He pointed at the stool. "Sit you down, girl. Tell me of your family."

Rosalind sat down gratefully. Her knees trembled more now than when she'd played her first part. "I lived with my grandsire, Pastor Broome. He is all the family I have."

"What of your father and your mother?"

Rosalind told Sir Robert of her mother's early death and of the death of her father in Spain. "He sailed with Lord Essex to fight the Spanish enemy," she said proudly.

Cecil's question was chill. "Did he?"

Then the girl recalled that this gentle-seeming little man was Essex's greatest enemy in all England. She was pleased when he didn't ask her anything about the earl. She was no longer devoted to Essex, but all the same she did not wish to harm him. He had not harmed her. To him, she was simply another Londoner who admired him.

Cecil went on, "You have no uncles and no cousins?"

Rosalind said, "Not to my knowledge. If I have, I have never seen them. My grandfather had an older brother in Sussex." Then she told the story of the ancient quarrel that had separated the brothers many years before her birth.

He asked next, "How did you come to London?"

Rosalind told him what she had told Pope but did not speak of her weeks at Moll's house in Whitefriars.

"And you became a player, deceiving even the other players."

"Aye, Sir Robert."

"And not one of them knew you to be a maiden?"

"No."

He shook his head and spoke sternly. "You are aware that you have gone against the Queen's law in playing parts. You have also broken God's law. There is a passage in the Bible that forbids women to array themselves as men."

"I know the passage." Rosalind lifted her chin. "It should be forbidden for men to array themselves as women, but boy players do."

He nodded at her. "Aye, that is said to be a disgrace too. Many pious men and women consider this custom also to be an abomination." Jolting her, he asked suddenly, "What was the trade of your grandfather's older brother? Was he a pastor also?"

"No, he held land of his own." Once more Rosalind was wary. Her grandfather would not want her to disgrace his family by being known as a thief and as a player. She would not tell Cecil that her grandfather was the brother of a noble lord.

"Was he a farmer then, Mistress Broome?"

"Aye, a farmer." Rosalind asked in turn, "Who is Master Fenchurch?"

"No friend to you, my girl."

Rosalind cried out, "But I have never harmed him!"

"So he tells me. He learned that you were supposed to have stolen a book and that you were a maid playing as a lad. He did his duty by the Queen to trip you up." Cecil pulled a piece of paper toward him, then reached for the inkhorn and a quill.

"I will look into the charge that you stole the book. As for your playing parts in the Lord Chamberlain's Company, I am well satisfied that it is fact. I can trust to the evidence of my own eyes. On that charge you *will* be held."

"I cannot go to Master Pope's house?"

"No, you will never return there. Nor do I think you will go back to Cowley."

"Where do I go then?" Rosalind got up in terror.

Cecil finished writing, folded the paper, and called out, "Guard."

The door was flung open instantly, and the chief of the guard came in to take the paper. Cecil spoke to him. "See to it that this girl is conducted to Sir John Peyton. I have written instructions for him in regard to her." Cecil fixed sharp brilliant eyes on Rosalind's face. "Mistress Broome, you are to go with this man at once. I am sending you to a very safe place. When I have got to the bottom of several matters, you will know."

Rosalind curtseyed, fighting a flood of tears. One of the five prisons in Southwark! This is what he meant by a "very safe place." Men and women who were shut up in them either died of fever or went to the gallows as Ned and Helen, the kyncheon coves, had for stealing a cup and a purse, though they had never succeeded in getting either object.

Conveyed by guards, Rosalind was taken out of the palace by torchlight and down to the moonlit Thames. Four guards crowded into a boat with her, no gaudy red, blue, and gold royal barge this time but a small covered boat. The six rowers took the boat quickly from the wharf and into the center of the river. The watermen rowed in silence, so skilled that their oars made almost no splash. Aye, they travelled to Southwark, the girl told herself unhappily, as she looked out the little opening next to her bench. They kept to the south bank of the stream passing Richmond Palace and Mortlake. Soon they went past the great looming shapes of the theaters and Bear Garden toward London Bridge, a thing of huge black arches over the Thames. Rosalind stared wistfully at the Globe, where she would never play another part, and she started to weep in truth.

Suddenly the Queen's boat changed its course. The watermen sent it scooting to the middle of the Thames, then under the middle arch of the great bridge. Sliding over on her bench, Rosalind looked out the opening at that side.

Ahead of her in the moonlight loomed the most fearful place in all England, the Tower of London, where noble folk were executed. Rosalind caught her breath in a sob. Was the Queen's Secretary sending her to the Tower, where people were tortured for information? There the Queen herself had been imprisoned as a young woman and her own mother beheaded, when Elizabeth was a very small child. Surely she didn't deserve the Tower of London for playing parts. Had it been such a terrible crime that she was to be kept in a stone dungeon and perhaps beheaded for it? Not even the Earl of Essex, Cecil's enemy, was imprisoned there.

Her worst fear came true when the boat's bow grated on the stone steps of the Tower. Two guards lifted Rosalind up by the elbows and took her out of the boat onto the slime-covered stairs. In front of her was the most infamous iron gate in all England, the water gate to the river, better known as the Traitor's Gate. Behind it were more guards with torches. Two were opening the water gate. Her feet slipping on the green ooze of the steps, escorted by two of the Queen's guards from Windsor, Rosalind was led through the gate into the Tower of London.

As it closed behind her with a sound of terrible finality, her knees gave way and she collapsed onto the dry stone stairs beyond the gate. She knew dimly that someone was carrying her a distance. Then she heard a door open and the voices of men and a woman. Next she was shifted to someone else's arms and was carried up more steps and placed upon something that creaked under her weight. Footsteps retreated and a door shut. Rosalind felt herself lifted by the waist and something set to her lips.

The woman's voice told her, "Drink this."

Rosalind opened her eyes and looked into the troubled face of a woman who was attempting to smile at her. She was neither young nor old and wore a cap of blue velvet trimmed with gold lace. Her fair hair was finely dressed. She was surely no prisoner.

"Who are you, my lady?" asked the girl.

"Lady Dorothy Peyton, wife to the Lieutenant of the Tower. This is a posset. Drink it. It will give you strength."

Rosalind twisted her head away. No, she would not drink anything this woman gave her. She was not a prisoner. This woman was her keeper.

Lady Peyton said, "I do not seek to poison you, Mistress Broome."

"I am a prisoner here," Rosalind said.

"Tush, you are to be held in our house, not in the White Tower or any other of the towers here. Sir Robert is not sending you to a dungeon."

Rosalind took a sip from the sugary posset and muttered, "Many have died here all the same."

"Many have, indeed," repeated Lady Dorothy. "Many have left here also—the Queen among them." She was no longer smiling. "My husband has been told by Sir Robert's letter the guard brought him that you have played parts in the new theater in Southwark and that you are a maiden, not a lad. You have passed yourself off as a boy."

"Aye, I do not see why it is such a very great crime."

"Some think it is. Do you wear a wig now? I see that your face is very painted. Did you come from playing a part?"

"Aye, at Windsor Castle."

"I have brought a cloth to wash your face. It has been set on the carved chest with a basin. Is your hair shorn as a boy's under that wig you wear?"

"Yes, my lady."

"Then you'd best wear the wig at all times. Have you women's clothing here in London?"

"No, naught but doublet and hose at Master Pope's house in Southwark."

"Ah, the player." Lady Dorothy got up. "I will see to it that you have bodice, sleeves, and petticoats at once. In the meantime, you must wear what you have. I have brought you a bedgown of my own. It is on the foot of the bed. Now finish drinking the posset, then sleep. It is late."

Lady Peyton went out of the chamber, shutting the door behind her and bolting it. Then the key turned in the lock.

Rosalind drained the posset while she looked around the small chamber. It was a pleasant room with a bed canopied in dark blue damask, two chests, and a window seat. She got up to look out the casement windows. It was black midnight outside. No moonlight seemed to enter these walls at this hour. The windows were tight shut, seemingly bolted across from the outside. Moreover, she was three stories above the ground, in an attic chamber, she guessed. She recalled being carried up a number of flights of steps.

She went back to the bed again. While she wiped off her player's paint and took off her auburn red wig and clothing, she asked herself if she must remain day and night in this room. What would she see from her windows in the morning? The gray, grim fortress that was the Tower of London? Would she spend the rest of her life looking at its ominous stones? She had passed it many times on her travels about

London with Dickon, the jostler, and with the players. They had told her that London had many Queen's prisons but only the "great lords and ladies" were sent to the Tower. If so, why was she here?

In the morning she went to kneel in the window seat and look out. What she saw made her spirits rise. The main building of the Tower of London was to the far right of the window. But directly in front of her was something far more pleasant: a broad green lawn rimmed by ordinary timber-framed houses. On the lawn were three children, two girls and a boy, all younger than herself. The girls were throwing a ball back and forth. The boy was chasing a large black bird, one of the famous ravens of the Tower. As Rosalind watched, a dark-haired woman came out of a house. She sent the girls inside but shoved the boy ahead of her out of Rosalind's view. He went with great unwillingness. She guessed he was being sent off to school. Did the dread Tower have a school as well as housewives and children inside its walls? Or were this woman and the children prisoners like herself? Aye, children, two royal princes, had been sent to this terrible place, and they had never been heard of again.

Later, after she had dressed in the costume she had worn as Mistress Page in the play and had put on the wig, Lady Peyton unlocked the door, pushed back the bolt, and entered.

"You will come down to breakfast with me when Sir John has spoken with you."

Behind the woman stood the Lieutenant of the Tower. He was a big bearded man, thick-waisted and gray-haired.

Unlike the guards, he wore no red doublet embroidered with a golden Tudor rose on the breast. His clothing was of mouse-gray velvet. There were no keys at his belt and no fearsome thing of torture in his hands; not even a halberd did he carry.

While Lady Peyton waited, the man spoke to Rosalind, "Mistress Broome, the Queen has put you under my care. I must keep you here until her pleasure is done."

Afraid of him, Rosalind said falteringly, "I saw children on the lawn. May I go there, too, to walk? Are they prisoners?"

"Unless it is forbidden, you may when you are better garbed." He eyed her gaudy player's costume. Rosalind gathered by his measuring glance that he disapproved of its orange-tawny and scarlet colors. "Do not remove your wig," he told her. Then he left the room.

"Lady Peyton, shall I walk freely here?" Rosalind asked.

"No, you will be accompanied always by one of the yeomen of the Tower guard. They will tell you where you may walk." The woman shook her head. "I am told that you, a maiden, undertook to study fencing. You will not be permitted near to the weapons of the Tower armory. Tush." She clicked her tongue against the roof of her mouth. Her hand on the latch, she told the girl, "There is a guard outside your door and guards set before this house. Do not seek to escape. You cannot. Men who have tried to let themselves down over these walls on ropes have broken their necks." Suddenly she asked, "Can you read?"

"Aye, my lady."

"Excellent. This afternoon you shall read to me and I to you. Do you do needlework?"

"Not very well. My lady, who were the children I saw outside? Were they prisoners like me? I saw a boy and two girls."

Lady Peyton smiled. "They are the children of one of the guards. That small imp of a boy you must have seen is Peter Gibbons. He makes me remember our own son, who is grown to manhood now. How slowly our lad walked to school. Peter does not like school."

"Is there a school here?"

"No, Peter goes to school outside the Tower. His sisters are taught at home."

Rosalind asked, "My lady, do you have books in Latin here?"

The woman's smile broadened. "Latin! Aye, we do, indeed. Do you read Latin then?"

"Once I did. I have not read it for some time. I also read Greek."

"A scholar? I doubt if you had much need of Latin and Greek among the common players?"

"No."

"A lewd and vulgar lot, but the common people like them very well."

Rosalind couldn't help but say, "The Queen favors them, too."

"Ah, yes, the Queen." Lady Peyton's smile faded. "May I bring Peter to you sometimes to say his Latin lessons? I do not read Latin. No one here has time for him, and his mother does not know Latin either."

"I would like that."

From inside the doorway the woman said, "On the morrow you will have other garments. Sir Robert is to send them. I hope that he will send garb that is suitable. I will

bring Peter to you tonight, so you can make his acquaintance. He has no need to be afraid of you."

"Why should he fear me?"

"He fears other prisoners here. Those who are traitors
to the Queen."

"I am not a traitor." Rosalind thought with a shudder of
Queen Elizabeth's little black-currant eyes.

"Mistress Broome, you have said openly in taverns with
the players that you love the Earl of Essex. It has been
reported to my husband."

Thinking hard, Rosalind said very slowly, "Once I loved
him greatly, because my father served under him in Spain.
I have spoken to Lord Essex but twice. I told him that
second time that my father died at Cadiz for him, and he
was kind to me. But I am certain that he would not remember me at all today or that I called myself Robin Broome
and was a player."

"Do you love the Queen then?"

Rosalind answered, "The Queen, at least, has paid me
some true heed. She remembered me as a player lad, even
before Master Fenchurch accused me at her court."

Lady Peyton nodded. "The Queen remembers many
things. What she forgets, Sir Robert Cecil remembers." The
woman jerked her head. "Come down now. One of the
serving maids will make clean your room while we eat.
Then you can look at our library of books. My husband
will be pleased that you read Latin and Greek. It is not
common for a maiden to read these languages—only noble
ladies do. He tells me he wishes I could read them."

As Rosalind passed through the door in the lady's wake,
the guard outside looked unsmiling at her.

XI

THE PRICKLY BEAST

That evening Peter Gibbons was brought up to Rosalind's chamber. A pink-cheeked boy with round blue eyes and thick, light brown hair, he was a far cry from the thin, pale London kyncheon coves she had known in Whitefriars. It was difficult to believe that such a child had spent all of his life inside the Tower of London, but so Peter had. He had been born in the Tower and "might someday become a guard," following his father, though he did not like the "traitors to the Queen" who came there.

As soon as Lady Peyton had gone out of the room, he asked Rosalind, "You are not a traitor, are you?"

"No?"

"Are you greatly wicked?"

Rosalind smiled, something she would not have believed possible when she first saw the watergate to the Tower opening before her. The Peytons had not been unkind to her, though they made it clear that she was a prisoner, and she no longer feared a dungeon. "No, Peter."

He nodded very solemnly for such a small boy. He said, "My father said that you were a common player."

"Yes, I was."

"That was a wicked thing to do. Men say that players like you cause the plague in London Town. It is worse that you are a maiden and a player."

"Do you like puppet shows?"

"Oh, yes," he told her, pulling up the stool Lady Peyton had brought for him to Rosalind's window seat.

"Are puppet shows so very different from plays?"

"I do not know. I have never gone to a play. My father says they are evil." His face brightened. "I have seen lords aplenty and the Queen herself when she visits the Tower. Do you love her well?"

Rosalind didn't answer. Instead, she took his slate and crayon from him and said, "Peter, what is the Latin word for *love*?"

"*Amo*," he replied, then proudly added, "*amas, amat.*"

Until Lady Peyton came to fetch him, he studied Latin words with Rosalind and not once more did they speak of plays and the Queen.

The following day a guard came into her chamber with a wicker hamper of clothing. In it was a black cloak, petticoats of dark wool, two bodices, two stomachers, three kirtles, and four sets of sleeves. Everything was dull and somber—browns, blues, and grays—but on top of the garments lay something unusual, gleaming brightly. It was a wig of silver-gilt color. Rosalind guessed that Sir Robert Cecil had sent it, remembering the true color of her hair. The Queen had never seen her without a wig. He had, though. Twice she had doffed her cap to him in the gallery at Richmond Palace. She had not dreamed he would recall the color of her hair. Yet he had!

Two watchful guards escorted Rosalind in her new clothing and flaxen wig around the Tower that afternoon. Lady Peyton walked with her as well as the two sisters of Peter Gibbons. Peter had gone to his schoolmaster on Tower Hill, one of the girls told Rosalind. Peter left the Tower each day, either for school or to worship at Allhallows Barking Church not far away.

By bright sunlight the Tower of London was not quite so frightening, though the White Tower, the central building where prisoners were sometimes tortured, still overawed Rosalind. There were several other towers built right into the massive stone walls of the fortress. Peter's sisters, familiar with the Tower, ran ahead of Rosalind and Lady Peyton, their bright skirts fluttering in the breeze. They named the towers as they passed them—the Beauchamp Tower, the Flint Tower, the Cradle Tower, the Bell Tower, and the Bloody Tower. Taking Rosalind by both hands, they dragged her to the barred gate of the Tower known simply as the Tower-at-the-Gate to peer through it to the outside world. It led out onto a causeway over the deep water-filled ditch surrounding the outer walls. At the end of the causeway was another stone tower, which the older girl Penelope called the Middle Tower.

She said, "The Queen's beasts are on the other side of the Middle Tower."

Her sister Judith added, "Many beasts are there. Have you seen them, Mistress Broome?"

"No." Rosalind looked mournfully through the heavy grill of the gate that kept her prisoner.

"Perhaps you could visit them if the Lord Lieutenant would give you permission," said Penelope. She turned to Lady Peyton. "Can she visit the lions, my lady?"

Lady Peyton sighed. "I do not know, Penelope. I do not command here. You know that. The Queen does." She told Rosalind, "If you would like, I could ask my husband to write Sir Robert Cecil and ask where you may and may not walk. I warn you, though, more often than not Sir Robert refuses the requests of prisoners."

Rosalind said, "It is of no matter. Thank you." She started back toward the Lord Lieutenant's house, keeping her eyes averted as they passed the Traitor's Gate. She would walk from now on only on the Tower green, the broad lawn before the Lord Lieutenant's house or in his herb and flower garden next to the White Tower.

Penelope and Judith Gibbons ran laughing ahead of her as she and Lady Peyton walked together. Rosalind asked her, "What folk have lived in your house, my lady?"

"The Lord Lieutenant, as the king or queen appoints him to the post."

"What prisoners? What lords and ladies? Was the Queen held there when she was a girl?"

"No, Queen Elizabeth was held in the Bell Tower. Her mother was held in our house, though."

The Queen's mother! Rosalind shivered. She had heard often of Queen Anne Boleyn, who had had her head chopped off because her husband, King Henry VIII, had wanted to get rid of her to take a new wife.

"What chamber did she have?" Rosalind asked, her fingernails digging into her palms.

Lady Peyton put her hand on Rosalind's arm. "Not the bedchamber you sleep in, though she was held in the top of the house, I am told. It was a number of years before my time."

Rosalind plucked at the dark gray cloth of her kirtle

nervously as she looked over the sun-dappled lawn at the pleasant-appearing house. It appeared harmless, yet out of its front door a young queen of England had come surrounded by guards and gone to her death by a great sword and block not far away. Not even out of sight of the Lord Lieutenant's house.

"I am not a queen," she told Lady Peyton. "I do not understand why I am here and not held in a common prison. Do you know why? Can you tell me?"

"I do not know. And if I knew, I could not tell you without written permission from the Queen or her Secretary. Nor could my husband."

"Can my friends come to visit me?"

"That I can tell you, Mistress Broome. You are not to have visitors. In particular you are not to see players. My husband has received instructions from Sir Robert concerning this matter."

"Do the players know where I am?"

Lady Peyton said again, "I do not know."

Rosalind did not ask about the canting folk. It would be a very bold rogue, indeed, who would come into the Tower of London. Yet one man *would* be bold enough—Tom o' Bedlam or Master Compton, as he called himself at the Queen's court.

That night, after she had helped Peter with his lesson, Rosalind lay awake for a long time in her locked and bolted chamber. Her thoughts were fixed on Tom o'Bedlam and on the stranger, Fenchurch, who had known of the theft of Dr. Hornsby's book and that she was a girl. Who was he, and how had he learned so much about her?

A fortnight passed with Rosalind seeing no one but the

people who lived inside the Tower. When the weather was sunny, she walked on the green with Lady Peyton or Penelope and Judith Gibbons and her guards. When it rained, she stayed inside, reading to Lady Peyton while the woman embroidered.

On rainy days Rosalind looked forward greatly to Peter's visits. The woman and girls rarely left the Tower nor did the Lieutenant, who said little to Rosalind at meals nor much more to his wife. He was by nature a silent man. Peter was Rosalind's link to the city of London, and she prayed that his visits to her would not be forbidden.

One evening Peter came to her chamber with his eyes swollen red from weeping. His cheek was bruised and his lip cut.

"What's amiss?" she asked him, as he sat down on the stool.

"'Twas a boy I met on Tower Hill. He jostled me, knocked me down and sat on me, and yelled into my face. Then he struck me in the mouth. The boy with him laughed at me. Rogues, they were, canting men in rags. They stole my slate and hornbook. I want no lesson tonight."

Rosalind snatched at the remark that the boys were rogues. "Tell me of them, Peter. What did they say to you?"

"The boy with red hair asked me if I knew a girl named Rosalind."

"What did you tell him, Peter?"

"That I did. He caught me by the hair then and banged my head on the cobbles of the street till I told him she was Rosalind Broome." Peter looked fearful. "I should not have done so. I think he knew that I live here in the Tower."

Dickon! It was Dickon, thought Rosalind. He knew then

that she was held in the Tower of London. He would tell Moll and the Upright Man. Perhaps they could help her.

"Rosalind, the boy said more to me before he hit me on the cheek. He asked if you went to see the prickly beast."

"The prickly beast?"

"Aye, not the hedgehog, but the porpentine, a dread beast with quills worse than any hedgehog. 'Tis there with the lions, a wolf, some bears, and the tyger."

"I hear the beasts at night. They roar sometimes," said the girl. "Peter, this boy asked you if I had seen the porpentine?"

"Aye, the prickly beast. That is what some of us call the porpentine. Do not tell my father or Sir John or Lady Peyton that I have told you what the boy said. It would make them angry. They have said that I am to speak only of Latin to you."

"I will never tell them, Peter. Do not repeat to them what you have said to me. You will come to no harm from me."

As Peter called for the guard to let him out of the chamber because he was too ill for a lesson that night, Rosalind thought of the two little rogues. Could they be trying to help her? Yes, they must be. Had Moll or the Upright Man sent them to Peter Gibbons? She must find out. She must get permission to see the beasts.

The next morning she spoke with the Lieutenant of the Tower over breakfast of porridge, roast beef, bread, and small beer. "I have fed the ravens on the green, Sir John, but I have not seen the lions. Would you write for me to Sir Robert and ask him if I may go there?"

He finished chewing beef, washed it down with ale, and

said, "I will write him at once. The Queen and court are at Greenwich Palace now. I do not see why he should refuse you this."

Rosalind ventured, "Does he write you in regard to me?"

"He does not."

Five days later a messenger came riding to the Lord Lieutenant's house. He took letters from his gauntlet, saluted Peyton who came out to meet him, and rode off again while Rosalind watched from her window seat. She waited, hoping that the man had been sent by Sir Robert. In an hour's time she learned that he had indeed come from Greenwich Palace. Lady Peyton climbed up to her with a message that she could "visit the Queen's beasts." On the very next day, they would all go—Rosalind, Peter's sisters, and herself.

Rosalind could not sleep at all that night for excitement. She did not walk up and down her chamber. The Peytons slept below. She sat in her window seat either gazing up at the free stars or with her cheek against the cold windowpane. Would Dickon be there? She prayed that he would.

The menagerie was kept by a royal servant, the Master of the Queen's Bears and Apes, but the important man was not there to greet Londoners who came to gawk. Other keepers looked after the animals and maintained order, but they made way for the guards from the Tower, the woman, and the three girls. The animals were kept behind stout wooden lattices. Under a guard of three men this time Rosalind was escorted from cage to cage.

Londoners who had paid to see the animals stared at her and at Lady Peyton and the girls as if they could not decide who was the prisoner. Amused, Lady Peyton told Rosalind, "We are as great an entertainment as the lions. Come, let us see the porpentine. It is a very curious beast."

Rosalind glanced once at the prickly beast, a thing of gray and black quills all over its back, then peered around for Dickon. Her heart gave a great leap. There he was, crowding in close to her, then pushing directly in front of her. He jabbed her with his elbow and whispered softly, "I've a message for ye. Tom's not returned. The Upright Man's sent after him to find him."

An eye on the nearest guard, Rosalind whispered to him, "What of the players?"

"All fares well wi' them. Master Pope's well."

"How now?" one of Rosalind's guard suddenly shouted. He moved forward with his long bladed weapon, the halberd, pushing through the throng. Dickon took one look at its sharp bright edge, then wiggled his way out of the spot in front of the porpentine's cage. Like a bolt from a crossbow, he sped out, dodging among the moving crowd of Londoners. In an instant he had lost himself in the crowd of menagerie visitors.

"What did he say to you?" the guard demanded of Rosalind.

"He spoke to me of the prickly beast. That is all."

Lady Peyton came up. "I saw the boy. He was harmless, only a small rogue by the looks of him. Come, we will go back now."

"But we have not seen the wolf," lamented Judith.

"You can see the wolf another day." Falling into step with Rosalind, Lady Peyton asked, "What did the boy say to you?"

"He spoke to me of the prickly beast, asking me if I had ever seen an English hedgehog so very large as the porpentine. I said that I had not. That is all. I do not think Sir John or the Queen's Secretary would be interested in the porpentine, would they?"

Three nights after her visit to the menagerie Rosalind heard footsteps on her stairs. When her door was opened, Sir John Peyton came in, this time in his bedgown and robe. He held a candlestick and lighted candle in his hand. It threw great shadows on the wall of the chamber, but its dimness gave Rosalind time to reach for the fair wig on the chest next to her bed and jam it on, hoping that she had not got in on backwards. Also dressed in her robe and bedgown, Lady Peyton, looking worried, came in after her husband.

"You are to dress yourself at once, Mistress Broome," the man ordered. "Make all haste. My wife will aid you."

"What is it?" asked Rosalind, getting out of bed the moment Peyton had left.

"I do not know," said Lady Peyton. "You have been summoned. My husband will take you to the White Tower as soon as you and he have made ready."

The White Tower? Rosalind's teeth clamped together to stifle a cry. Why the largest, most important tower of them all? Her fingers trembled so she could not tie on the sleeves of her gown. The chore was done by Lady Peyton, who had no smile for her now.

Sir John was waiting with four guards at the foot of the stairs. He said nothing to her, only held open the door of the house. Walking with him, two halberdiers ahead and two behind, Rosalind went in a perspiration of terror to the

White Tower that was such a short distance away. She climbed its outside steps into a large stone chamber. A guard led them from there single file up winding steps so narrow that only one person at a time could use them. Aye, this was a fortress, indeed, built by a king of England hundreds of years before. Even one brave man with a sword could hold the stairs for a long time against all comers. By the time she had reached the top, Rosalind's heart felt nearly ready to burst. But at least, she told herself in her fright, she was climbing, not going down into some horrible black dungeon.

The guards led her and the Lieutenant of the Tower through what seemed to be a candle-lit chapel carved out of pale yellow stone into a small room leading off it. The door to this room was opened by a guard stationed outside it.

Rosalind saw Peyton bow, taking off his hat. He told her, "Make a curtsey." Then he preceded her inside, saying, "I have brought the girl as you requested."

Peyton bowed again and went out, leaving Rosalind staring at the Queen's Secretary. Sir Robert was sitting, dwarfed in an enormous chair, eating a leg of fowl and drinking wine from a silver cup set on a small table beside him. The cold stone room also held a bench and a wooden bed built against the wall, but not another object except for the straw on its floor. "Sit down, sit down," he motioned with the capon leg toward the bench. When Rosalind had sat down, he reached out to the plate beside him, found the other leg, and held it out to her.

"Eat while you may," he told her.

Rosalind took the food, then nearly dropped it. Was she about to be beheaded here and now? Worse things had happened in the White Tower, she suspected. "Wh- what?" she stammered.

"Eat while you may. Much of the time I am too busy to eat at all. I sup whenever and wherever I can. Eat. Do not prattle."

Eyeing the little man, Rosalind ate, though she had no appetite. Why had he got her out of bed? It must be midnight at least. What would bring Sir Robert here to the Tower? Was he now a prisoner of the Queen, too? But then prisoners did not give orders to the Lieutenant of the Tower.

He went from capon to white manchet bread, which he also shared with Rosalind. While she was eating her second piece of bread, choking it down, the door was opened once more. Rosalind gagged on the bread.

In the door frame stood the Upright Man of London, bowing and smiling, splendid in a popinjay-green satin doublet. His eyes flickered to Rosalind but once. He nodded a greeting to her, then fastened his gaze on the Queen's Secretary.

"Ah, Jack," said Sir Robert. "It took you long enough to obey my summons. What news have you now of Tom o' Bedlam?"

The leader of the rogues said, "He lies in gaol in Hertfordshire. They took him up for a vagabond."

Cecil let out a small sigh. "I shall see to it that he is released at once. I shall not need you further tonight, Jack. Next time when I summon you, come at once."

"Aye, Sir Robert." And the Upright Man was gone.

Rosalind sat with her hands on her knees, her eyes popping. First, she had seen Tom o' Bedlam, then the Upright Man of London speaking with the chief servant of the old Queen.

Cecil put down his wine cup with a noise that drew her attention to him. "Tell me, Rosalind Broome, what you know of the man who accused you at court, this Adam Fenchurch?"

"I know nothing of him. I have seen him twice, both times in your presence."

"Have you marked your resemblance to him?"

Rosalind shook her head. She recalled how the players had taken note of this fact at Richmond Palace, though. "No, but Master Burbage did. And others too."

Cecil grunted. "They would see such a thing. Mistress, it seems to me that the Upright Man knew you. How long did you live among the canting folk?"

Rosalind wanted to scream at him, "Must you know all things!" but she held back the words. Feeling defeated, she said, "I spent some weeks with them. I knew the Upright Man."

"And you knew Tom o' Bedlam well. You met him on the road in Oxfordshire and you knew him also in London, did you not? You knew him to be a rogue?"

"Aye." Rosalind looked down at her tight-clenched fists,

"Mistress Broome, you told me at Windsor that Tom o' Bedlam brought you to London, but you did not tell me that he brought you to the canting men of the town. Why did you not?"

"I did not wish to harm them. Some of them have befriended me."

He grunted again. "So the rogues are your friends and the players are not?"

Stung, Rosalind blurted, "No player comes here to the Tower to see me."

Cecil said in a sober fashion, "No, no player has. They

cannot. They do not know that you are here. But if it would please you to hear it, Master Thomas Pope visits the prisons every day in London and Southwark searching for you. No other player does this." He paused. "So you like the rogues? I am told that Moll Cutpurse sheared your head. Did you like that?"

"She did not cut my hair to harm me."

He put his fingers into his little beard. "The canting men did not frighten you. Did you feel yourself to be one of them?"

"Aye, they frightened me. The things they chose to teach me frightened me. I could never learn to do them well enough to suit them. But they made me most afraid when they talked so much of serving the Devil."

"Did they talk often of that?" To her surprise, he chuckled. "You had a country pastor for a grandsire and a humble pious old farmer for a great uncle in Sussex, did you not? Certainly you would fear the Devil." All at once he demanded, "Have you wondered how the canting men knew where you are held—in what prison?"

Rosalind could only nod her head in misery.

He went on, "The boy who spoke to you in the Tower four days past sent a message to you. Do not deny this. I know what the message was. It concerned Tom o' Bedlam, who has not yet returned from his travels."

Rosalind gasped. Dickon! He had caught Dickon, too, and had questioned him, perhaps tortured him. She would try to save him if she could. She lifted her head to stare directly into Cecil's watchful eyes. "The boy who spoke to me was my friend. He could have known where I was. The rogues see everything in London."

He laughed aloud. "So they do, mistress. At times they

serve the Devil well enough, almost as well as they served his father before him, though at other times they are difficult to control."

Rosalind flared, "I have heard that said before. I will say the same thing to you that I said to the rogues. The Devil has no father."

The little man's voice turned very cold. "My father served the Queen until his death two years past. I serve her today. Do you not know that I am nicknamed Robert the Devil?"

Rosalind put her hands to her mouth. This was the flesh-and-blood man that Tom o' Bedlam, the Upright Man, Moll, and Dickon served. And this Devil had put her into the Tower of London. How they feared him!

He asked, "Do you think I keep you safe here *only* because you may have stolen a book from an old scholar and because you, a maiden, were a player? You should thank me for what I do for you now."

Scarcely knowing what she said, Rosalind whispered into her hands, "I thank you, Sir Robert."

XII

MY LADY

Rosalind thought constantly in the days that followed of her conversation in the White Tower with Cecil. What had he meant by his questioning? She knew that he had come especially to see her. Sir John Peyton had informed her of this at breakfast the morning after he had conducted her to the Secretary. Soon after she had said "thank you" to him she had been dismissed and Sir Robert left the Tower at once to be rowed back to Greenwich Place, where the Queen still resided.

Neither of the Peytons nor the Gibbons children asked her about the visit, and Rosalind volunteered nothing. Sir Robert Cecil had not demanded her silence, but she felt she must keep it. Her babbling might harm Dickon or Moll, who were true friends. She was less sure of the friendship of Tom o' Bedlam or the Upright Man, who were clearly instruments of Sir Robert.

As for his being the Devil, that seemed to be truth indeed. How very much he knew of matters concerning her!

Ten days went by with Rosalind feeding the Tower

ravens, helping Peter with his Latin, and reading to Lady Peyton. Ironically one of the books she often read from was a copy of the very book Tom had stolen from her on the road to Cowley.

One summer evening while she was sitting in the window seat watching shadows the rising moon created on the green, Sir John Peyton came to her chamber. He said, "I am bid to take you to Richmond Palace on the morrow."

"Is it by order of the Queen's Secretary?"

"Aye, Mistress Broome, it is."

"Will I return here?"

"I know not. If you are to return, I will bring you back with me. I am to wait for you there. God give you good night."

"God give you good night also."

When he had gone and secured the door against her escape, Rosalind knelt down beside her bed to pray. She asked that she be spared returning to the Tower and for God's protection from Robert the Devil.

Not long after dawn Rosalind, cloaked and hooded against the river's mists, went out of the Traitor's Gate and into another closed boat. Peyton and four guards accompanied her into it and later into a closed wagon that took them over a rutty road to Richmond Palace. Rosalind had not looked out at Southwark and the Globe as they rowed up the Thames. She tried later not to remember her last visit to this huge stone palace, though the usher took them by the same route. She had been happy that night walking in red livery with the Lord Chamberlain's Company. How long ago it seemed that she had been Robin a Dale, the player.

And now she was Rosalind Broome, the Queen's prisoner!

The Secretary's antechamber was smaller here than at Windsor Castle. And there was no window seat or chair for anyone with shaking legs—or for Sir John Peyton. They were forced to stand.

But Rosalind did not have to wait long. Another usher led her alone through a little door into Sir Robert's closet, which was almost a replica of the one at Windsor.

This time he was not alone. A man stood in front of the Secretary's table, a man wearing a fine velvet doublet of murrey red. Rosalind recognized him by his fair hair. He was Master Fenchurch.

He swung about at once when the usher announced her as, "Mistress Broome." Rosalind saw the look of absolute astonishment on his face as he gaped at her. Then he turned abruptly back to Cecil.

Rosalind looked, too, at the Secretary. He was smiling and said, "No, Master Fenchurch! The girl was not hanged as a common thief as I told you a fortnight past. She is very much alive. I think you and she should know one another better. Master Fenchurch, this is your kinswoman, Lady Rosalind, the Baroness of Broome!"

"*What do you say?*" demanded Fenchurch. He looked at Rosalind again while she stared in disbelief at him. Her kinsman! *This man?* This man who sought to have her hanged.

Cecil went on, "Aye, Lady Rosalind, Master Fenchurch. I have looked into her family. Her grandfather was the brother of Lord Broome of Farn in Sussex. Both old men are now dead. She is the legal heir—not you."

Rosalind moved backward to the wall of the tiny room.

Her head felt about to explode. A baroness! And her grandfather dead! She started to slide down the wall but her progress was stopped by a bench.

As if from a great distance she heard Fenchurch saying, "She is my kinswoman, you say? I did not know that there was another heir but myself. Then I am not Lord Broome, it seems. I was mistaken. I regret that I accused my kinswoman of a crime, though God knows she was a player and she did steal a costly book."

"But did she steal, Master Fenchurch?" Cecil asked. "And do not tell me that you did not know that there was a female heir who had a better claim to the barony than yourself. You had enquiry made in Cowley before I did. You sent a man there. I have been told of him. I have heard, too, of him elsewhere. Master Fenchurch, I say that you sought again and again to rid yourself of this girl here in London."

"I did not!" Fenchurch protested.

"But you did, indeed." Cecil paused and then cried out one word, "Guard!"

When two guards came through a door on the right, they brought a man with them. Rosalind took one glance at him, jumped up, and put her hand over her mouth to stifle a scream. The man was black-bearded and swarthy. He was the very man who had come at her with a dagger among the properties of the Globe.

Sir Robert told her, "Do not be frightened, my lady. You need not tell me that you recognize this man. I can see that you do. He murdered the little player lad, thinking he was you. He came later to the Globe to find you. I have had enquiry made regarding him." Cecil took up a piece of paper and read from it. "Martin Sclater, is it not? And you are Master Fenchurch's servingman? You were found in his house in Saint Albans, were you not?"

"Aye," Sclater mumbled, looking at his shoes.

Cecil commanded, "Show me your hands. Many folk have spoken of them."

Rosalind looked on in horror as Sclater spread his scarred hands on the top of Cecil's table. This man must be the one Dickon and the jostler had met and the trumpeter at the Globe had seen. Yes, he had murdered little Davey.

Rosalind saw the color drain out of Fenchurch's face until it was gray-white. He shouted, "Lady Rosalind or no, the girl is a common thief!"

"Master Fenchurch," said the Secretary thinly, "she is not a common thief. She may be a noble thief but not a common one. As for you, you are a very great rogue. I am shamed that you once served me. You serve me no longer."

"I am not a rogue!" Fenchurch cried.

"No, you are not. I did not have the right of it. Forgive me. You are less than a rogue. You did not even serve the Devil honorably. Rogues serve me better. You are a foul creature." Cecil gestured with one tiny white hand. "Guards, conduct these men to the custody of the Lieutenant of the Tower, who is waiting in the antechamber. He will know how to get the entire truth out of them."

"There is no truth to it at all!" shouted Fenchurch, as he was taken by the arms and pulled away by the guards.

As the door shut behind him and Sclater, Cecil asked Rosalind, "Now, my lady, what do you have to say for yourself? Or, as the Queen is rumored to have said, has the cat got your tongue?"

Rosalind could only nod. The sight of Martin Sclater

had been a third blow to her. She still could not realize that she was a noble lady or that her grandfather was dead or that she'd seen her would-be murderer.

"Do not faint. I have not the time today for that folly," Cecil told her sharply. "You had the courage to be a player, to bear parts when you were a maiden not a lad. Show courage now. I have not done with you. Guard!" he cried. "Bring a cup of wine for Lady Rosalind and then usher in the two gentlemen who are waiting."

Rosalind drank the wine gratefully, glad of the support of the little bench. Her knees might not hold her if she tried to stand again. She looked up once she had finished the wine and saw two more men enter, bowing and doffing their hats. She knew them both.

One was Tom o' Bedlam resplendent in a black-and-yellow doublet and hose and the other Dr. Hornsby in his long black scholar's gown. Rosalind forgot about her knees. She got up and ran to her grandfather's old friend to embrace him. As he patted her on the back, he told her, "Do not fret, Rosalind. Your grandfather did not believe you stole my book, nor do I."

"I did not steal it."

"No, you did not steal it," agreed Sir Robert. "Another did, did he not, Master Compton?"

Tom said calmly, "He did, and he will make amends."

"It would be wise of him to do so. He is not so ill paid for his services," remarked the Secretary dryly. He turned to Rosalind. "Good Master Compton here went to Sussex, to Oxfordshire, and then to Saint Albans on your behalf, Lady Rosalind. Or so he tells me."

"*Lady Rosalind!*" Dr. Hornsby exploded.

"Aye, sir, this is Lady Rosalind, the Baroness of Broome. Take my word for it that she is. Bow to her ladyship, gentlemen."

Dr. Hornsby, looking amazed, bowed to Rosalind; then Tom o' Bedlam bowed. Hornsby seemed shaken by the disclosure, but Tom was grinning broadly at her.

Cecil went on, "Master Compton gathered news that convinced me of several things and convinced the College of Heralds that this girl was the heir to the barony. She shall soon be proclaimed and her claim be acknowledged by the Queen. What do you have to say now to Master Compton, my lady? You owe him very much."

"I thank you, Master Compton," Rosalind told Tom. "Were you beaten in Saint Albans?" she asked.

"Not at all, though I was in gaol."

"A pity that you were not. I thank you for all I have learned with you and through you."

Cecil nodded toward Hornsby and Tom. "I wish to speak to Lady Rosalind alone now. Await me outside. I will meet further with the two of you later today."

Both men bowed, first to Rosalind, then to Sir Robert, and left the closet. Sir Robert got up from his chair and bowed to her also. He did so with polite graveness, but somehow he seemed to mock her, Rosalind thought. Then he sat down again. "Now let us get to the remainder of our business together, my lady."

"Must I go back to the Tower?" she dared ask him.

"I hope that you will not. It depends on what you say to me. There are two matters I must take up with you."

Rosalind interrupted, "I did not steal the book. You know that."

"Yes, I know. That is not one of the matters. As you may remember, I once said to you that I sent you to the Tower to keep you safe. Why do you think I sent you to such a place?"

"Because you thought I stole a book and had been a player, though I was a girl."

He laughed while he crumpled the paper in his fist. "No, it was indeed to keep you safe. I sought to keep you under lock and key, and I could have sent you to any common prison in London or Southwark. But I chose the strongest prison of all, not because of your crimes but because I did not want Master Fenchurch to find you. I knew that he had claimed the barony. I marked his resemblance to you and wondered at it as I had wondered before at his great impatience to be proclaimed Lord Broome. I had told the heralds to move very slowly in the matter of his claim. When I heard him call you Rosalind Broome, I wondered even more. And then I learned, from certain of my good servants, of the dark man who sought you in various places and of the death of the player lad and of the attack upon you in the playhouse. I wondered who would profit from your death. Who would try to kill a common player? And why?"

Rosalind asked, "You heard of me from the canting men?"

Robert the Devil had a very sweet smile. He nodded, then went on, "They gave me more news of you than that, though I must say it took some hard questioning. You went with two other children who were also rogues to a goldsmith's house in Blackfriars to thieve, did you not, my lady? You were to steal roses from the garden. The other two were to steal a cup and a purse of silver. The City Watch surprised you. You ran and got away, and later to disguise you the mort of the Upright Man cut off your hair so you could pass as a boy and hoodwink the Watch. As for your becoming a player, that had naught to do with the canting men."

Rosalind drooped again. This man did know everything. "I took no roses from the garden."

"Ah, but you had it in mind to. You went there with the intent to steal. You trespassed behind walls. This is a crime. I can ask the Queen to forgive you for it and believe she will, rather than have you stand trial before the House of Lords."

"Stand trial?" Rosalind was stunned at the thought. She flared in anger, "I stole nothing at all. I have never stolen."

"No matter. You have been very troublesome to the Queen, who has things of more import than your madcap behavior. You are to be sent to Oxford, not with Dr. Hornsby but in a wagon of the Queen's. You are to be educated there in the things that befit your station, the things that will prepare you for a noble marriage."

Rosalind jumped up again. "I do not want to marry. I want to go back to the players."

"Sit down." He rapped the table with his fist. "You cannot. If you are discovered playing parts again or associating with players, it will go very hard with them and with you. The Queen was greatly offended at your being with them when you were a common wench. What will she say if you, a noblewoman, play parts before the public?"

Rosalind plunked down onto the bench once more. "I will not marry."

He soothed her. "When the time comes, I will try to manage it so you may wed a young lord of your own choice. Today, though, you will go to the house of Lady Margaret Forster."

Rosalind slumped. She muttered, "My grandfather wished me to go to her."

"So good Master Compton learned in Cowley, and Dr. Hornsby confirms it. If you had gone willingly to Lady Margaret's house in the first place, none of this would have taken place, though of course Master Fenchurch might still have attempted to have you murdered." As Rosalind wiped her eyes with the hem of her skirt, Cecil told her coldly, "I told you not to faint and you did not. You must not weep now. Do not grieve for your grandfather here. Later would please me better and take less of my time today. God's bones, do you think you are the only person in England? Others wait outside to have audience with me. If you live peaceably for a time with Lady Margaret, you can take comfort in the thought that you will be pleasing your grandfather, who is no doubt in heaven. I was told that he was very godly."

Rosalind giggled. The Devil was talking about heaven and godliness. She asked, "Will I be a prisoner there, too, with Lady Margaret?"

"That is her decision. She will watch you closely, I am certain. You will not come to London without the Queen's permission. You will see your estates in Sussex, to be sure, but you will not come to your house here in London until you are old enough to comport yourself with discretion and not run after rogues and players."

"I have a house in London!"

"You do. Lord Broome had a house in Seething Lane. He had not lived there for many years, but he kept servants in it."

"Was he so rich that he could do that?"

"He was, indeed. And now you are very rich."

"Is my London house in Seething Lane a large one?"

"Aye."

Rosalind's face brightened. "Would it have a chamber large enough for plays to be performed there?"

"I am certain that it would." He pointed at her. "You must never play parts in public. It is not only forbidden to maidens but it is forbidden to all of the nobility."

"In private then?" Aye, she *would* play parts in her own house. *She would!*

He sighed. "Perhaps. But it may not delight the Queen to hear it."

"The Queen plays the virginals, lute, and cithern, does she not? Master Pope says she is a good performer."

"She does, but she is not paid to perform."

"Is the Queen pleased in *all things?*" Rosalind asked, tossing her head. An instant later she clutched at her slipping wig.

"She is. I try to see to that, Lady Rosalind. Now get up. You must go to the Queen and then be on your way to Oxford. Lady Margaret knows that you are coming to her at last. She has written to me that you will also have lessons from Dr. Hornsby. She says you are something of a scholar, though I find this difficult to believe. It appears to me that you are more fitted to the life of a rogue than that of a scholar."

Rosalind noted how her hands trembled. She had to see

the Queen once more. She hoped the third time would be the very last. She feared the old woman greatly. She tried to play at lightheartedness. "Sir Robert, I heard Tom o' Bedlam speak of flowers, of loosestrife and pimpernels, to an innkeeper once. What did he mean? Do you know?"

"Babble," he said, "naught but babble. The man must have played at seeming a lunatic. Only madman's prattling."

No, Rosalind told herself. It was not babble. She debated whether to tell the Queen's Secretary that Tom had said the same words to the Upright Man. She decided not to. "Loosestrife." What did it mean?

And suddenly she felt she knew. The key lay in the other words—the red witch and the Devil. The Devil was clearly the man she was now talking to. If he was the Devil, then the red witch was the Queen. The Queen's natural hair had been red when she was a girl. "Loosestrife" could mean exactly what it said, "Begin war." Who would go to war against the Queen? Why should Tom o' Bedlam be asking such a question? Only one man would do so—the Earl of Essex. Tom and the rogues gathered news of Essex, the Queen's and Cecil's enemy. Tom roamed often around the countryside. The innkeeper's wife in Oxford had said he listened at inn doors and to stranger's talk in common rooms. She knew that the rogues had many ears in London Town. These people informed the Secretary of men's and women's opinions throughout the land regarding possible enemies to the Queen. They were the Queen's spies. She supposed there must be many of them. Fenchurch, too, had been a spy for Cecil.

Rosalind felt a coldness rising in her breast. She was

afraid for Lord Essex, but more for herself. She also feared
for Master Pope and Dame Gillet. She must take great care
not to offend the Queen and Sir Robert. She must protect
her friends.

As Cecil stood aside at the door to let her precede him
into a gallery, Rosalind asked, "What of Master Pope and
his household and Master Burbage? They have done no
wrong."

"I am satisfied as to that, my lady. Master Pope and
Master Burbage will be told that you died in gaol of fever.
If you see them again, they will not know you as Robin a
Dale, but as Lady Rosalind Broome. I am certain that you
are expert enough a player to convince them that you were
never associated with them."

"But, Sir Robert." Rosalind stopped in the center of the
deserted gallery, her voice echoing. "Some of the players
heard Master Fenchurch call me Rosalind Broome at
Windsor Castle. They knew me first as Robin Broome.
They know the name Broome."

"They will have short memories, my lady. Even Master
Shakespeare, the most clever of them all, will forget you.
I can promise you that. They will not offend you or me or
the Queen. I think they can be convinced not to presume
upon their old friendship with Robin a Dale. They are not
stupid men. They are more clever than many other men
who have better educations and very high rank and are
overambitious."

As the little man started off again, Rosalind knew he
spoke of the Earl of Essex. She knew he would not call
him by name. He went on as if he had guessed her
thoughts. "Look to the plight of one great lord. He pro-

voked the Queen. Learn from him. Do not ask too much of her or of me. It will not be granted. And already you are no favorite of hers."

Rosalind said thoughtfully, "Aye, Sir Robert."

Two galleries away from his audience chamber Rosalind found the Queen sitting in the center of a circle of six ladies-in-waiting, listening to one of them singing a ballad of a maiden who had wed a rich old man rather than the poor young man who loved her well.

Rosalind curtseyed while Sir Robert bowed, then waited with him until the ballad was finished and the Queen had waved her ladies out of the tapestried chamber. The ladies left in a slithering of white silk skirts, and now the Queen, her Secretary, and Rosalind were alone.

The old woman garbed today in cloth of ice-blue and silver brocade glared at Rosalind and shook her head in irritation.

Sir Robert spoke first. "Your Majesty, I have brought you Lady Rosalind as you commanded. I have done with her. She goes to Lady Margaret Forster's house today." He whispered to Rosalind, "Go up to her. Go to your knees before her and kiss her hand. It is required of you."

Slowly the girl went forward, shaking as she always did in the old woman's terrible presence. Yes, the Queen was looking very angry. She said, "Master Rosalind, is it? Is it still Master Rosalind with you, my flouting wench?"

"No, Your Majesty." Rosalind went down on her knees and took one of the Queen's long perfumed hands and kissed it. "I am now the Lady Rosalind Broome."

"So I have been told. And no credit you are to me at all!" The Queen drew back her hand and struck Rosalind on the side of the head, making her clutch again at the wig. "Go to the country, learn to comport yourself well, and let your hair grow to a fitting length. God's bones, passing as a lad and playing parts on the stage. I wonder at your boldness and your insolence."

Holding her cheek, Rosalind said nothing. But in her heart she wondered still what was so evil in her playing parts. She, a girl, had played girls and women. She did not play men!

"Leave us, my elf," the old woman called out to Cecil. He bowed and backed away, closing the door softly behind him.

Rosalind felt that her heart beat in her mouth. What would the Queen do to her now that they were alone? Strike her again? What happened surprised her. She felt the Queen's cool fingers on her chin and her head being tilted upward so she had to look into the Queen's wrinkled, painted face. Was the Queen about to spit on her? Master Pope had said the Queen had once spat angrily into a courtier's face.

Elizabeth was smiling. She asked quietly, "Did you enjoy being a player? Tell me the truth."

"I did, Your Majesty."

"Aye, a maiden who has spirit might like playing very well. It is pleasant to be cried out at by people who love you. I know that well."

Rosalind could smile now, too. "Your Majesty, you do not have to fear that people will throw dead cats at you."

The Queen's face twisted as she said, "No, I fear men who will take my throne from me. What is a dead cat to that?" She went on, while Rosalind thought again of the

Earl of Essex, "Tell me something more. Did you like play-ing the part of a boy day and night? I am told that the players never guessed you were not a lad. I find that passing strange."

"They did not, Your Majesty. I found it pleasant to play a boy."

"You liked it more than being what you truly are, a maid?"

"To tell the truth I did."

Old Elizabeth sighed. "So would I, I think. I did not have the chance to play at being a man. I would never have chosen to be born a wench." She looked away from Rosalind. "Do you know, Lady Broome, how I speak of myself?"

"No, Your Majesty."

The Queen grinned, showing her few black teeth. "I do not say that I am a Queen. I name myself a Prince. Do you like that?"

"Aye, Your Majesty." The Queen was no longer so fear-some. In her heart Rosalind suspected she might even learn to give her love to her as she once had to Essex. No, he should not seek to take the old woman's throne from her.

Queen Elizabeth asked, "Lady Rosalind, do you pledge yourself to serve me faithfully?"

"I will serve you."

"Good." Elizabeth tapped Rosalind on the cheek with a flick of her fingers. "I accept your homage to me. Now, arise, and get you to Oxford, Master Rosalind."

AUTHORS' NOTES

The temptation is ever with us to make our notes as long as our novel inasmuch as we take equal delight in them. However, we shall resist temptation and confine our remarks to what is "real."

Rosalind Broome could have become a peeress without her realizing it. In the age of plague and smallpox epidemics entire families could be wiped out in a matter of days and the family title go to what the Scots call a "far-out kinsman." (Living in humble circumstances is no real bar to inheritance of peerages.) One early seventeenth-century earl, for instance, was an aged country pastor whose daughters, it was claimed, knew more of milking cows than of fine needlework.

We have tried to describe Oxford University as it was during Elizabethan times, with its social distinctions and rules for student behavior. Students were forbidden to attend plays performed by common players in innyards, though students acted in university productions themselves. Dr. Hornsby is fictional, but he is based on a real master of one of the Oxford colleges, a tartar of a man who ruled not only faculty and students but once reprimanded the Queen in her presence in a public address.

LONDON

London in Shakespeare's day was a small city but a very lively and prosperous one, filled with shops and famous taverns. It had various districts favored by certain classes of citizens and those of certain occupations. Tradesmen clustered in special streets. The thieves stayed chiefly to Whitefriars. Many rich lived in Blackfriars. Noblemen had great houses on the north bank of the Thames. In 1600, the Royal Exchange was one of London's finest sights. Not so, Saint Paul's Church. Its middle aisle was a fashionable rendezvous and the church itself a place of sometimes sordid business.

SOUTHWARK

Southwark, across the Thames from London but linked by house-covered London Bridge and a navy of watermen, was an unsavory place for the most part. Because public playhouses and bear gardens could not legally exist within the city of London itself, they were to be found there as well as north of London in Holywell Fields.

Many respectable people resided in Southwark, however, Shakespeare himself for a time as well as Thomas Pope.

THE CANTING MEN

London, like all great cities, has always had an underworld. In 1600, the Upright Man ruled the rogues who were, as we have described them, involved in the specific sorts of crimes for which they were best suited. *Nip, angler, prigger of prauncers*, etc., were actual terms of the day. Certain taverns were the haunts of the canting men and avoided by the knowledgeable, respectable citizen.

An Abraham Man, a wandering beggar feigning madness, was a canting man as was the self-wounded clapperdudgeon.

The paragraph we have put into the mouth of the Upright Man lists some of the actual crimes for which a person could be hanged during Elizabeth's long reign. Thieves kept special schools for children they recruited to crime. There was such a school on Smart's Quay.

As to the exact sixteenth-century patois of the canting men, we have not made great efforts to reproduce their talk with one another. It would never be understood by modern young readers, but we have tried to give a flavor of it. (The same difficulty is experienced with modern Cockney speech. During our years of residence in London we were greatly entertained to hear non-Cockney Londoners complain of the overslangy incomprehensibility of Cockney talk, which is a famous cant of its own.)

THE PLAYERS

The amount of material written about the Elizabethan theater is staggering. Reading all of it would take a lifetime. We have used many books in researching *Master Rosalind*, but not *all* of the literature. We've relied on what university-based Shakespearean scholars of our acquaintance recommended to us.

To begin with, the Puritans, who were gaining strength

during the reign of Elizabeth I, detested plays and players, considering them heathen and greatly wicked. Some Englishmen actually believed that the production of plays led to outbreaks of the plague as God's punishment of the wicked. Yet most Londoners were not Puritans, and plays were performed to the joy of audiences, who were very willing to stand for hours throughout the performance or to sit on uncomfortable stools and benches.

We have attempted to describe the Curtain in Holywell Fields, the demolition of its sister playhouse, the Theatre (a fact in 1598), and the building of the Globe from the timbers of the Theatre. We have tried briefly to give young readers a view of what the playhouses looked like inside and outside and how the playgoers conducted themselves. The description of one particular stage and of the list of properties is factual, though somewhat condensed for the purposes of the novel.

Boys played girls' and women's parts. Women did not appear on the public stage until the 1660's, and then were considered scandalous sights. If men players were considered wicked, women players were more severely censured. Throughout the eighteenth and nineteenth centuries a stigma clung to actresses as evil and immoral people.

During the reign of Elizabeth I there were companies composed wholly of boy players. Promising boys were even kidnapped and made into players. Ten was considered a prime age for a boy to begin a career as an actor's apprentice. At times the players' companies were often desperate for boy players, since they grew up at varying speeds. Some lads played women's parts to the age of twenty; others, maturing earlier, had to stop at thirteen or fourteen. Many boy players went on to become adult players.

It is true that players were often excellent swordsmen. They dressed in dazzling fashion (sometimes because noblemen who were their patrons sent them their cast-off clothing). However, although a few players became wealthy men, they were never truly respectable citizens in the minds of some Londoners.

Various Elizabethan nobles sponsored companies of players. Chiefly the companies gave plays in their own playhouses, but they were always at the command of the Queen's Master of Revels and had to travel to whatever palace Queen Elizabeth and her court were occupying at the moment.

Players were generally careful not to offend the Queen, their all-powerful patroness, though at times they ran afoul of her, especially when the play offered reflected too sharply on kingship.

PLAYS

In this book we have attempted to write of Shakespeare's plays, putting them in chronological order, though Shakespearean scholars are not in much agreement as to their order. *The Taming of the Shrew,* we gather, would have been performed prior to 1598 and then played again later. Plays were sometimes "revived." *Midsummer Night's Dream* was an older play, as our Master Gulliford says. Some scholars claim that *Henry V* was the first play produced at the Globe, so we have set it as the first in which our Rosalind appears. *As You Like It* was supposedly first performed in 1599.

Having been successful as the heroine of *As You Like It* does not mean, in Elizabethan theater, that our Rosalind would automatically play lead roles forever. The players' companies then did not follow the Hollywood star system. (For that matter they do not follow it today in England. Actors can be leads one week and supporting players the next week.) So our Rosalind could have gone on to much lesser parts in *Julius Caesar* and *The Merry Wives of Windsor,* later plays.

Modern-day scholars have attempted to assign parts in Shakespeare's plays to various historical actors. We have followed their suggestions, accordingly casting Burbage, Pope, and Shakespeare himself into roles they might truly have played. We have also bewigged our heroine according to scholars' ideas of the coloring of such and such a character. We understand that heroines were usually blonde or red-haired—lesser female roles called for darker wigs.

Bewigged boy players who played women were also painted with cosmetics to look like actual ladies of Elizabethan times. Some of the paints they used were dangerously poisonous, but they were the same cosmetics favored by court ladies, including the Queen, and often worn to cover the ugly scars of smallpox and ravages of age.

THE COURT

The court of Elizabeth I was constantly on the move from late spring till autumn. The Queen's entire household was packed into wagons and sent from royal palace to palace and noble house to noble house. Elizabeth and her court sought to escape the plague, which was always to be found in rat- and flea-infested London.

Elizabeth enjoyed honoring the less wealthy of her nobles. Her court could literally eat a poor nobleman out of house and home and drive him to the brink of bankruptcy. He was always forced to entertain his Queen and her entourage in a very lavish manner. The visited nobleman could console himself with the thought that he had pleased his Queen and that she might shower future honors on him. This did not always occur. A relation of Oliver Cromwell, for instance, was financially ruined by a three-day visit of Elizabeth's successor to the throne, King James I, and his touring court.

THE TOWER OF LONDON

London and Southwark had a number of prisons in the 1600's—common prisons for common people, that is. The Tower of London, already a very old fortress by 1600, was not for ordinary citizens but for those accused of crimes that threatened the Queen—chiefly treason. Hence, the powerful, noble, and famous were sent there when they were not kept under "house arrest."

The Tower of London is not one tower but a number of them. Only the White Tower, which is not built into the walls, stands alone as the chief one. Today one building houses the crown jewels of England, which are on display under glass for the public to gasp at.

The lieutenants of the Tower were appointed by the incumbent king. In 1600, Sir John Peyton was the actual Lieutenant, and his wife was named Dorothy. Our scarcely dangerous prisoner, Rosalind Broome, would very likely have been held in the Lieutenant's lodgings and could live with his family. Women prisoners, some of whom were eventually beheaded on Tower green, were lodged with the Lord Lieutenant and others of the guard.

THE PEOPLE IN THIS BOOK

Elizabth I, shrewed, vain, witty, and courageous was

herself once a prisoner in the Tower of London and in danger of execution while her hostile older sister, Mary, ruled. On the death of Mary, Elizabeth became Queen and did, indeed, refer to herself in public speeches as a "prince." We think she would have chosen to be a king, though she set the tone for all Englishwomen as the fashion plate and epitome of lovely womanhood. In later years Elizabeth who had a fabulous wardrobe of wigs, gowns, and jewels wore generally, "moonlight colors." She had favorites among her nobles, but she was ever the ruler, jealous of her power, might, and rights. During her long reign (1558-1603) she was forced to dispose of a number of people who threatened her throne, but she did so most unwillingly. For all her quick temper she was not inhumane or bloodthirsty.

She favored scholarship, learning, art, music, masques, and plays. She often had groups of common (professional) players perform before her at her various residences. A legend says that she commissioned Shakespeare to write the comedy *The Merry Wives of Windsor* to amuse her, because she wanted to see a certain comic character who had appeared in an earlier play in the "throes of love." Elizabeth was said to have preferred comedies to tragedies and did not like plays that showed kings in a bad light.

Robert Devereux, second Earl of Essex, was the old Queen's last favorite as well as a kinsman of hers. Years younger than she, he had none of her wisdom and cleverness. He was handsome, rash, temperamental, and convinced that he could rule as well as she. He overstepped all bounds as a military leader in Ireland and as a courtier in England. It is fact that the Queen once boxed his ears in a fit of temper at his impertinence.

Essex knew his finest hour when he led an expedition against Spain in 1596. In January, 1601, thinking wrongly that he could get the people of London to support him against the Queen, he gathered malcontents about him and came out in the city in open revolt. The people did not rise to support him. He was arrested, taken to the Tower of London, tried as a traitor, sentenced, and a month later beheaded. (One of the Towers of London today is called the Devereux tower because Essex was held there.)

Sir Robert Cecil was in fact nicknamed Robert the Devil among his enemies. On the death of his father, who had been Queen Elizabeth's principal secretary, Sir Robert succeeded to the post at the early age of thirty-five. His father had built up a very good espionage system throughout England to ascertain ahead of time how and where threats to the Queen were developing. Sir Robert fell heir to this network and used it cleverly, keeping the identity of his many agents even from one another.

He was a tiny man, a hunchback. Although he was called Devil by some, the Queen at times referred affectionately to him as her "elf." Cecil was not a personally cruel individual. He served the Queen well as he served the man who came to the throne after her, King James I. Sir Robert died in 1612, as the Earl of Salisbury.

Richard Burbage, the younger son of a player father, began his very distinguished career as an actor around 1584 after serving an apprenticeship as a boy player. Ten years later he was with the Lord Chamberlain's Company, playing heroic leads such as Romeo in *Romeo and Juliet* and the king in *Richard III*. Later he was to play the parts of Macbeth, Hamlet, and Othello. Multitalented, Richard Burbage was also a well-known painter. Married, with seven children of his own, Burbage, too, took in boy-player trainees. He died in 1619.

Thomas Pope, a bachelor and the "large clown," lived in Southwark with his housekeeper, Dame Gillet Willingson. Pope played parent over a number of years to various orphaned children. His protection and teaching of our Rosalind is in character. Pope played in Denmark, and in 1594 he joined the Lord Chamberlain's Company. Reputedly wealthy, he owned three houses in Southwark and a fifth share of the Globe. The actor, who claimed to be of gentle birth, retired from the stage in 1603.

Will Kemp, who also resided in Southwark, was the "small clown." By 1590, he was a famed comedian, and in 1594 was with the Lord Chamberlain's Company. He also had a share in the Globe but sold it in 1599. On a bet he went marathon dancing to Norwich and from there to France, Germany, and Italy. In 1601, he rejoined Burbage and others but soon left them for another company. There is no record of him after 1603.

Henry Condell, who lived in London with his wife Rebecca and their nine children, was a player of varied roles. He seems to have been more versatile than most of the actors he performed with. One of the younger adult players of the Lord Chamberlain's Company in 1600, Condell died in 1627.

Ben Jonson was born about 1573. An actor, as well as a writer of satirical comedies, Jonson specialized in in loud, heroic, and melodramatic roles. Though his plays lacked the depth, great poetry, and marvelous humanness of Shakespeare's, they were popular in London. His play *Volpone* is often played nowadays.

Jonson, to say the very least, was a turbulent man in a turbulent age. One of his plays so offended Queen Elizabeth that he went to prison because of it. At another time he was imprisoned because he killed a player in a duel. He was branded on the thumb for his very unruly behavior. In 1599, he was associated as a playwright with Burbage's company. Outliving almost all of the men of the Lord Chamberlain's Company, Jonson died in 1637.

William Shakespeare (1564-1616) is far too famous to need even a brief review of his life story—or what little is known of it for fact—told again. His chief renown is, of course, as a great poet and playwright. His career as a player is less well remembered, though it is on record that he played parts in his own and in other men's plays. In his own time he was revered for his gentleness and kindness. So we do not feel he is out of character to have befriended our Rosalind.

SOURCES

We have used a large number of books in writing *Master Rosalind*.

To describe Elizabethan London, for instance, we used, among others, *London in the Time of the Tudors* by Sir Walter Besant; *The Pageant of Elizabethan England* by

Elizabeth Burton; *Elizabethan Life in Town and Country* by M. St. Clare Byrne; *Shakespeare's England,* (2 volumes) of the Clarendon Press; *The Elizabethan Journals,* edited by G. B. Harrison; *The English People on the Eve of Colonization* by William Notestein; and *Shakespeare's London* by Fairman Ordish.

The material on the canting men is chiefly drawn from a fascinating section of one of the two volumes of *Shakespeare's England.*

In gathering material on Queen Elizabeth and her court we used: *The Reign of Elizabeth* by J. B. Black; *Queen Elizabeth First* by J. E. Neale; *The Earl of Essex* by G. B. Harrison; and *The Second Cecil* by P. M. Handover.

In writing of theatrical matters we have chiefly relied on: *William Shakespeare, a Study of Facts and Problems* by Sir E. K. Chambers and the *Elizabethan Stage* by the same noted author.

Other books valuable to our research were: *The Organization and Personnel of the Shakespearean Company* by Thomas Whitefield Baldwin; *Shakespeare the Player* by Alexander Cargill; *Shakespeare of London* by Marchette Chute; *A Shakespeare Companion* by F. E. Halliday; *Shakespeare at Work 1592-1603* by G. B. Harrison; *Ben Jonson* (4 volumes) by C. H. Herford and Percy Simpson; *The Child Actors* by Harold Hillebrand; *Shakespeare's Theatre* and *The Globe Restored,* both by C. Walter Hodges; *Essays on Shakespeare and Elizabethan Drama* by Richard Hosley; *Shakespeare's Wooden O* by Leslie Hotson; *Shakespeare and The Actors* by Arthur Colby Sprague; and *Shakespeare's Dramatic Heritage* by G. W. G. Wickham.

As for the conversations used throughout the novel, we have relied on the *Shorter Oxford English Dictionary on Historical Principles,* edited by C. T. Onions.

A number of people suggested bibliographic material to us. Some are professors of English, others of drama. We are indebted to Dr. Douglas Cook, Dr. William Elton, Dr. Eugene R. Purpus, Dr. Richard Risso, and Dr. Catherine Shaw. We also wish to express our gratitude to librarians Dorothea Berry and John Maxwell of the University of California, Riverside library.

John and Patricia Beatty

June, 1973

Both John and Patricia Beatty were born in Portland, Oregon, and went to Reed College there. After graduation Mrs. Beatty studied at the University of Washington in Seattle, and Dr. Beatty received his M.A. from Stanford University and his Ph.D. from the University of Washington. He is now a professor at the University of California, his subject being English history of the seventeenth and eighteenth centuries.

The Beattys were married in 1950 and later lived in Wilmington, Delaware, and London, England. Dr. Beatty served in the United States Army in World War II, in the European Theater. He is the holder of the Silver Star and Purple Heart medals and the Combat Infantryman's Badge. Mrs. Beatty has taught high-school English and history and has also held a position as a science and technical librarian. Recently she taught Writing Fiction for Children in the Extension Department of the University of California, Los Angeles. She has had a number of novels published by Morrow about the American West.

John and Patricia Beatty now live in Southern California with their teen-age daughter, Ann Alexandra.